The Art of Murder in Brussels

Matt Borne

More stories by Matt Borne

The Cipher of Eden

In the shadowy ruins beneath Jerusalem, Dr. Sarah Kensington, a lauded biblical archaeologist, uncovers an enigmatic copper scroll, sparking the ire of a sinister religious sect.

Simultaneously, Vatican-based Jesuit scholar, Father Anthony Miller, unearths a millenia-old conspiracy linking the Church to a concealed truth about Eden.

When their paths collide in a heart-stopping quest, they must decrypt an ancient cipher, navigate a deadly labyrinth of religious politics, occultism, and a string of grisly murders, all while eluding a relentless assassin.

Join Sarah and Anthony in a breathtaking thriller, where they grapple with blurred lines of faith, history, and power, racing against time to thwart an apocalypse and unmask the chilling secrets held by "The Guardians of Eden."

The Cipher of Eden: where myth and reality merge, catapulting the world towards the brink of utter chaos.

Available in print, as e-book and audiobook.

The Luigi Ferro Series by Matt Borne

Luigi Ferro, Private Investigator

Luigi Ferro is no ordinary Private Investigator; he's a connoisseur of life's finer things, all while solving the gritty mysteries that plague the citizens of San Marino and the surrounding Italy. From his cliffside office overlooking the town, he juggles a love for women, a penchant for fine wine, and a taste for gin garnished with a slice of lime.

But don't let his indulgences fool you. When it comes to untangling the complex webs of his clients' dilemmas, Luigi is as sharp as the cliffs are steep. With a keen eye and a mind that's even keener, he's the man you want to unravel your mysteries, all while savoring the zest of life.

Available in print, as e-books and audiobooks.

Note. This is a work of fiction, and even if the places and people of this story have existed or still exist, the events are the brainchild of the author.

The Art of Murder in Brussels
By Matt Borne
Copyright © 2024
Cover design by Mats Ingelborn
Art by Midjourney
ISBN print: 978-91-89822-56-6
ISBN e-book: 978-91-89822-57-3
Published by Yabot AB, Sweden, 2024

1

A slender silhouette framed by the morning light stood at the window overlooking the cobblestone artery of Brussels' old quarter. The dawn spilt its golden hue over the rooftops as if to varnish the city with a promise of discoveries. With each sip of his robust coffee, which he cradled in a china cup that was itself an antique, Nicolas De Wever savoured not just the rich blend but the quietude of the awakening street below.

"The quiet before the bustle," he mused to himself, inhaling the rich aroma of his brew. The bitter notes of the coffee mingled with the earthy scent of antiquity that rose from his shop—an olfactory reminder of his life's passion.

Nicolas was a solitary figure against the backdrop of his book-laden flat, his tailored suit impeccably fitted as if it were an extension of his being. He set down the china cup with a soft clink and descended the winding staircase to the heart of his world.

"Good morning, my treasures," he whispered reverently as he pushed open the door to the shop. Sunbeams pierced the storefront windows, casting a glow upon a tapestry of cultural relics. He ran a slender finger along the spine of a leather-bound tome, feeling the years etched into its surface.

"A new day to find you new homes," he continued,

speaking to each piece as though they were cherished guests in his care.

With deliberate steps, he navigated through the shop, which was an embodiment of his refined taste. Flemish oil paintings watched over Louis XVI furniture, while Art Nouveau vases kept company with delicate Chinese porcelain. Each item was a testament to Nicolas' eye for beauty—a curator's symphony played out in wood, canvas, and glass.

"Perhaps today is the day you'll catch someone's eye," he said, adjusting the angle of an 18th-century mirror, ensuring it reflected the most fetching view of its Baroque companions.

His movements were gentle and respectful, the care of a guardian preserving history. And yet, behind those sharp blue eyes swirled thoughts of provenance and the silent tales these objects held. The weight of their secrets pressed upon his mind, their quiet whispers promising the thrill of discovery.

"Every scratch, every patina, a chapter in a story," he thought as he unlocked the shop door, returning to the familiar embrace of his antiques. Perhaps that is love enough for one lifetime. He took a miniature painting he had stored in the back room and started to examine it.

After an hour, the bell above the door jingled, signalling the start of the day's commerce. Nicolas straightened, adopting the expected professional facade, yet his curiosity never waned. It was this insatiable hunger for art's mysteries that fueled his reputation among the cognoscenti of Brussels, a passion evident to any who crossed the threshold of his establishment.

"Welcome," he greeted the early visitors, who sauntered in with a large parcel under one arm.

The man placed it on the desk and opened it.

Nicolas De Wever's fingers traced the contours of the eighteenth-century brass lamp that had just been presented to him. The client, eager for appraisal, watched as Nicolas's sharp blue eyes narrowed, scrutinising the curvilinear forms and intricate embossing.

"Remarkable," he murmured, his voice a soft baritone that resonated with authority. The lion's head motifs guarding the stem were not lost on him, nor was the gentle patina whispering tales of candlelit chambers and whispered confidences.

"Found it in my grandmother's attic," the client said, watching Nicolas's examination with a mix of impatience and hope.

"Indeed?" Nicolas replied, barely lifting his gaze. He adjusted his glasses and leaned closer, his sharp blue eyes scrutinising the minute engravings that danced along the lamp's stem—a pastoral scene etched with such care it could have been the work of a grand master's hand.

"Look here," he said, gesturing with a tapered finger to the intricate details. "The narrative within this metalwork—I suspect it's Flemish. The craftsmanship is exquisite." His touch was feather-light as if afraid to disturb the story locked within the artefact.

"Is it worth much?" the client asked, shifting from one foot to the other.

"Value," Nicolas began, straightening up, "is often subjective in our world. But to the right collector, I dare say, it would be worth some three, maybe four, thousand Euros." A smile played on his lips, one reserved for those brief moments when history whispered its secrets to him. "Would you like me to find a new owner for it?"

The man met Nicolas' gaze. "Four thousand Euros?"

"Maybe, but we can agree on a lowest price of three," said Nicolas.

"And what would your commission be?"

"If I am to sell it for you, I take thirty percent, but if you want me to buy it I can offer you 1500 cash today," explained Nicolas calmly.

The man thought for a while before taking the cash.

After delicately placing the lamp aside, Nicolas returned his attention to the painting that seemed to command its sphere of silence within the shop. The canvas, modest in size but arresting in presence, depicted an autumnal scene—a storm of russet leaves against a brooding sky. Nicolas's fingertips hovered a hair's breadth from the surface, afraid to mar the brushstrokes that seemed almost alive under the shop's gentle lighting.

*

"Good morning, Monsieur De Wever," came a cheerful voice from the door. Isabella Leclerc, his assistant, stepped into the shop with the grace of someone who had found her calling among the relics of yesteryear. She was a vision of youthful exuberance juxtaposed against the gravitas of the collection she tended to with such care.

"Good morning, Isabella, punctual as ever," Nicolas remarked with an approving nod. Her presence brought a refreshing dynamic to the shop, her eager eyes seeing both history and the future in their curated confines.

"Wouldn't dream of being late when art awaits," she replied, a playful twinkle in her eye. She glanced around the room, her gaze lingering on the newly acquired brass lamp. "I see you've made an exquisite addition since yesterday."

"Indeed," he confirmed, following her gaze to the eighteenth-century lamp he had been inspecting earlier. "Your discernment grows keener with each day," he praised, aware of how vital her fresh perspective was to the lifeblood of the gallery.

"Thank you, Nicolas." She blushed slightly at the compliment. "It's all thanks to your guidance."

He watched as Isabella began her morning ritual, delicately dusting the shelves with the tenderness one might use to cradle a newborn. Her slender hands moved with confidence, a testament to the knowledge she had accrued under his tutelage.

"Any appointments today that I should be aware of?" Nicolas queried, retrieving a ledger from beneath the counter.

"Just the usual consultations and a pick-up for

Madame Durand's vase," she responded, pausing to consult the planner. "Oh, and Claire Dubois mentioned she might stop by to discuss the upcoming exhibition."

"Ah, Claire." His mind briefly wandered to his neighbour and fellow art lover, her gallery a well-known fixture across the street. Their professional camaraderie was tinged with mutual respect forged over years of amiable rivalry.

"Shall I prepare in the back room then?" Isabella asked, snapping him back to the present.

"Please do," he assented, already turning his attention to the figures in the ledger. He penned notes in the margins, the numbers whispering stories of provenance and prestige.

As Isabella disappeared into the back, Nicolas allowed himself a moment's reflection. Though solitary outside these walls, his life was rich with the silent companionship of bygone eras. Here, amidst the tangible echoes of history, he found solace. Yet, part of him wondered if his dedication to preserving the past had come at the expense of a present yet fully lived.

"Nicolas," Isabella called from the other room, her voice pulling him from his reverie, "the Vernet painting— any thoughts on where it should be displayed?"

"Let us find it a place where it commands the room yet invites intimacy," he called back, his expertise subconsciously dictating the perfect balance required.

"Understood," she replied, her tone infused with

the same passion that animated the very walls of their sanctuary.

The door chime rang, announcing the arrival of the next patron. Nicolas straightened his suit jacket and prepared to welcome them.

The young woman who entered immediately captured his attention, a figure so striking that her presence seemed almost anachronistic against the backdrop of his shop's historic elegance. Her petite shape was accentuated by a flamboyantly styled ensemble, a whirlwind of colours and patterns that clashed in an eye-catching and slightly disconcerting manner. Despite the chaotic blend of her attire, there was something undeniably modern about her, a walking testament to the eclectic spirit of contemporary fashion.

Yet, as Nicolas's gaze lingered, he couldn't help but notice the peculiarities of her figure—the slimness of her build, lacking the curves typically associated with a woman's hips, juxtaposed with a surprisingly prominent bosom. It was an observation that made him slightly uncomfortable, not because of any judgment on his part but because he was acutely aware of the implications of his scrutiny. In the world of antiques, where every detail told a story, Nicolas was trained to observe, but the realisation that his observational habits extended to his visitors stirred a sense of intrusiveness he didn't quite appreciate.

As she moved towards Nicolas between ancient artefacts and timeless treasures, her gait was confident yet carried a hint of something indefinable—a mismatch between her vibrant appearance and the air of disarray that clung to her. It was as though she was a living, breathing piece of modern art, deliberately placed among the relics of the past to challenge or perhaps to complement them.

Her shoes were equally eye-catching – red ankle boots with a glossy finish and high heels, providing a sharp contrast to the soft, historical carpets covering the shop floor. Her slim legs were clad in mustard-yellow tights topped with a short black leather skirt. She wore a boldly patterned blouse – a kaleidoscope of colours that clashed delightfully with the statement necklace, an oversized piece with chunky, colourful beads that captured the essence of her vibrant personality. Her wrists jangled with an assortment of bracelets, each seemingly telling a story of its own, from intricate beaded designs to sleek, metallic bangles.

Nicolas found himself both intrigued and slightly bewildered by this enigmatic visitor. While admirable, her bold expression of personal style seemed to amplify the contrast between the world outside his shop's doors and the timeless sanctuary he had cultivated within. The juxtaposition was stark, a vivid reminder of the ever-evolving nature of beauty and expression. Yet, it also underscored the universal desire to stand out, to make one's mark in any era.

"Good morning," Nicolas greeted the newcomer with

the same courteous smile he offered to every patron, regardless of their appearance. "How may I assist you?"

The woman, unabashed by her unconventional appearance, stepped forward with confidence.

"I'm looking for something unique, perhaps a painting or a piece of furniture that stands out," she said, her eyes scanning the room with an unexpectedly discerning gaze.

Nicolas nodded, guiding her through the items on display. He showed her a collection of exclusive paintings, each with its own rich history and artistic merit. The woman listened as Nicolas described a nineteenth-century landscape, a fine example of the Romantic period's allure. Her questions were pointed and knowledgeable, revealing an unexpected familiarity with art history.

Her interest then shifted to furniture. "What about that commode over there?" she asked, pointing to an exquisite French piece from the Louis XV period, its intricate marquetry glistening under the soft lighting.

"Ah, a remarkable choice," Nicolas replied, his eyes lighting up with enthusiasm. "This particular commode is a fine example of the Rococo style, crafted during the reign of Louis XV. Notice the detailed marquetry—each veneer carefully selected to create this floral motif."

She leaned closer, her eyes tracing the curves and patterns of the wood. "It's beautiful," she murmured. "Does it have a story?"

"Indeed, it does," Nicolas said, leaning in with a conspiratorial air. "This piece was once housed in a chateau in the Loire Valley. It's not just a piece of furniture; it's a piece of history. The craftsmanship speaks of an era where artistry was as valued as functionality."

She ran her fingers gently over the surface, her touch reverent.

"It's more than I expected to find here," she admitted. "I was looking for something unique, but this... this is a treasure."

Nicolas smiled, pleased by her appreciation. "It's often those who least resemble connoisseurs who possess the deepest appreciation for art," he observed.

Her gaze met his, no longer flamboyant but imbued with a newfound respect. "I work for a law firm," she revealed. "I'm redecorating their reception area. I want something that stands out, makes a statement about who they are—sophistication and history."

"Then you have certainly chosen well," Nicolas affirmed. "This commode will not just stand out; it will tell a story and add depth and character to your space."

She nodded, decisive in her posture. "I'll take it. And those paintings we discussed earlier."

The transaction was significant, reflecting both the quality of the pieces and the discernment of the buyer.

As the woman arranged for the delivery of her purchases, Nicolas felt a surge of satisfaction. Once again, he had matched the right pieces with the right patron, a skill he prided himself on. The woman, now a representative of a distinguished law firm, thanked Nicolas for his assistance and expertise.

As Nicolas prepared the paperwork, he reflected on the encounter. Beneath her unconventional exterior, the woman had an eye for beauty, a sense that transcended her outward appearance. It was a reminder of the timeless allure of art – capable of bridging worlds, connecting disparate souls through the appreciation of beauty and craftsmanship.

With the deal concluded, Nicolas decided to enjoy a leisurely lunch, a small celebration of the day's success.

"I'll take a lunch walk," he announced to Isabella as he left the comforting cocoon of the shop, the soft chime of the door echoing into the crisp Brussels day. The narrow street, lined with cobblestones worn smooth by time, cradled a symphony of hushed conversations and the aromatic whisper of fresh pastries from nearby patisseries.

"Nicolas," called a voice, slicing through the air with the precision of a well-crafted sculpture. It was Claire Dubois, emerging from the sweeping archway of her own art sanctuary across the street. Her gallery, an institution as revered as Nicolas's, was a testament to their kindred spirits in the realm of fine art.

"Ah, bonjour, Claire," he greeted her, his voice carrying the warmth of shared respect. "A bit brisk today, isn't it?"

"Indeed," she replied, wrapping her cashmere shawl tighter around her shoulders. "I trust your latest acquisitions are as exquisite as ever?"

"Only the finest, as you well know." His smile was one of quiet confidence, a man assured of his standing within the intricate tapestry of the art world. A passing glance between them conveyed volumes; they were custodians of history's treasures, each piece a silent guardian of bygone eras.

"Your reputation is impeccable, Nicolas," Claire said, her hazel eyes glinting with mock admiration. "It's a rare gift to see the true worth in things overlooked by others."

"Thank you, Claire," Nicolas replied with the same amount of mock gratitude.

"Let's discuss the exhibition after lunch," Claire ended, retreating into her domain. Nicolas turned his gaze skyward, where the sun cast a golden hue upon the ornate facades of the surrounding buildings. He mused on the solitary nature of his existence, his life an intricate mosaic of antiques and artistry, each piece resonating with stories of love and loss.

2

Nicolas headed towards Brussels' Grand Place. The midday sun in March casted a warm glow over the historic square. It was a tapestry of architectural marvels and, as always, buzzing with the lively chatter of tourists. Mobile cameras captured visitors' memories against the backdrop of ornate guild houses and the grandeur of the Town Hall.

He manoeuvred through the crowd with a practised ease, but suddenly, his steps came to an abrupt halt. A gathering crowd had enveloped the area; their attention riveted on a solitary figure commanding the stage. It was Pascal Charlie, a nationalist politician known for his fiery rhetoric and fervent beliefs in the destiny of Belgium.

Pascal's voice, charged with emotion, cut through the air.

"We stand here, in the shadows of giants, our forefathers, like the great Jean-Joseph Charlie!" he exclaimed, referencing the legendary hero of the Belgian Revolution. His words, infused with an enthusiasm for the past, captivated the audience.

"We must remember their sacrifice, for it is their blood that has coloured the fabric of our nation!" Pascal continued, his hands gesturing emphatically.

Nicolas, usually distant from such political discourse,

found himself trapped by the raw energy of Pascal's speech.

Despite the magnetism of Pascal's oratory, Nicolas felt a stirring of unease.

"Belgium for the Belgians, as it was meant to be!" Pascal shouted, his voice echoing off the ancient buildings. This brand of nationalism, intense and exclusive, didn't sit well with Nicolas, who believed in a Belgium enriched by diversity.

He watched as the crowd swayed with every word, a sea of nodding heads and clenched fists.

"Our heritage, our identity, must be preserved against the tides of change!" Pascal cried out, his face aglow with passion.

Nicolas's gaze lingered on the speaker, his mind grappling with a conflict of admiration and disagreement. The homage to Jean-Joseph Charlie and the Revolution was stirring. Still, the underlying message of Pascal's words painted a picture of a divided future far removed from the inclusive society Nicolas cherished.

As the speech reached its climax and the crowd erupted into thunderous applause, Nicolas quietly retreated from the square, deep in thought. Pascal Charlie's voice, still resonant in the air, left him contemplating the delicate dance between honouring the past and embracing a future that welcomed all. The Grand Place, a testament to Belgium's layered history, had once again become the stage for a moment that would linger in the memory of its onlookers, including Nicolas, who walked away with a mind heavy with reflection.

Continuing his stroll, he reached the famous Manneken Pis. A queue of tourists, each eager for a photograph with the iconic statue, snaked around the corner. Nicolas paused momentarily, observing the fascination and joy on the faces of those seeing the whimsical statue for the first time.

At the neighbouring street, Lievevrouwbroerstraat, the market day was in full swing. Stalls brimming with vibrant flowers, fresh produce, and artisanal crafts lined the street. The air was filled with the mingling scents of street food and the melodious sounds of traders announcing their goods to passers-by.

Nicolas strolled through the market, each step a reminder of the city's vibrant pulse, a blend of tradition and the bustling rhythm of contemporary life. In these streets, every corner held a story, and every stone whispered a piece of history. Nicolas, an antique dealer with a soul attuned to the past, felt profoundly at home, or to be completely honest, he loved a local market.

"Antiques! Get your genuine antiques here!" cried a vendor, his voice a smooth baritone that cut through the clamour.

Nicolas glanced at the array of goods on display—a hodgepodge of brass candlesticks, porcelain dolls, and yellowed lace—none worthy of more than a cursory glance. He moved on, but not without noting the earnest desperation in the vendor's eyes; it was a look he knew all too well in this trade where authenticity was king and fakes abounded.

"Fresh strawberries, monsieur?" A plump fruit seller held forward a sample, her smile bright against the backdrop of vibrant reds and greens.

"No, thank you," Nicolas replied, his tone polite yet distant. The sweetness of the fruit held no allure compared to the thrill of unearthing a hidden gem amongst the residue of the past.

As he navigated the labyrinth of stalls, Nicolas's sharp blue eyes scrutinised each object, searching for the telltale signs of age and craftsmanship that signified true value. Most items were mere trinkets, unworthy of his expertise, but the possibility—the sheer potential of discovering something remarkable—kept his pulse lightly tapping at the edge of excitement.

The market was like a mosaic: vibrant textiles juxtaposed with rustic woodwork and gleaming metalware alongside leather-bound books whose spines whispered tales of forgotten lore.

But mostly junk, he thought, his heart quietly lamenting the disposable culture that had infiltrated even the sanctum of antiquity. Yet, hope was not lost, for experience had taught him that even in the most mundane of settings, greatness could be concealed, waiting for the right eye to perceive it.

His lunch break dwindling, Nicolas prepared to return to his shop on Korte Boterstraat, already feeling the comforting embrace of its hushed interior, where every artefact spoke of a grand and intimate world.

"Nicolas, how do you fare today?" The familiar voice belonged to a fellow antiquarian whose gaze was equally discerning.

"Ah, Henri, as well as one can amidst such chaos," Nicolas replied, a satisfied smile on his lips.

His gaze drifted across the haphazard assembly of oil paintings and watercolours. This visual cacophony seemed to blend into one unremarkable blur. His fingers brushed against the textured fabrics of canvas and paper, a tactile Morse code transmitting tales of mediocrity until they paused, hovering with an involuntary tremor of curiosity.

"It's a bit dreary for your taste, right?" Henri commented, his breath thick of tobacco.

It was a small painting, nestled between its larger, more ostentatious cousins, its surface dulled by time and neglect. But Nicolas was not captivated by the painting but by its frame. This elegant, ornate piece hinted at a rich history. The frame's intricate carvings and the subtle patina spoke of craftsmanship that could be worth hundreds. Yet, Nicolas chose to mask his genuine interest.

"Oh, it's not for me," he lied smoothly, a practised ease in his tone. "I have a client who's been looking for something with these exact colours for her taverna. It's more about the ambience than the art itself. Mind if I..." His words trailed off as he reached out, fingers grazing the frame with the reverence of a man who had unearthed a relic of forgotten significance.

"Go ahead." Henri shrugged, his interest piqued by the sudden solemnity that had overtaken the otherwise indifferent customer.

Nicolas held the painting up in the air, tilting his head to consider the piece from various angles. Sunlight caught at the edges, hinting at hidden depths beneath the grime. It was signed "G D". It was no masterpiece but spoke of craftsmanship and a time when artisans imbued even the simplest trinket with a breath of their soul.

"Let's see if we can't agree on a price that reflects its apparent worth, shall we?" Nicolas suggested, his voice steady, betraying none of the anticipation that now lapped at the shores of his composure.

"Twenty euros," Henri declared, with an assertive nod towards the painting in Nicolas' hands.

"Twenty seems ambitious for such a… modest piece," Nicolas replied, fingers brushing over the frame's surface as if feeling for the artist's intent hidden beneath centuries of dust.

"Modest? You just said that you already have a client for it," Henri protested, puffing up slightly at the challenge to his wares.

"Nothing is certain," Nicolas replied. "And the market for such paintings is limited if she backs out. I'd be taking quite the gamble."

"Eighteen, then." The vendor's eyes darted to Nicolas' face, searching for a tell.

"Ten," Nicolas countered smoothly, his heart maintaining its rhythm despite the silent drumroll of anticipation. He knew the dance well—each step, each turn of phrase, a familiar tune.

"Ten!" Henri scoffed, yet a glint of concession flickered behind his outrage. "Fifteen, and you're robbing me blind."

"Twelve, and I'm still the one being generous." Nicolas' voice remained even, but inside, the current of excitement began to surge. The possibility of unveiling a treasure from within the ordinary fueled him, a secret thrill known only to those who seek beauty in the overlooked.

"Fourteen, and not a cent less. You've got yourself a deal, Nicolas." Henri extended a grudging hand.

"Thirteen," Nicolas said firmly, extending his hand, "and we have an accord."

The vendor hesitated, a battle of profit and pride waging behind his furrowed brow. Finally, he grasped Nicolas' hand, sealing the pact.

"Thirteen, then," he muttered, and Nicolas couldn't help but detect the slightest note of admiration amidst the resignation.

Money exchanged hands—a trivial amount for what might be harboured within the frame—and Nicolas wrapped the acquisition in brown paper with meticulous care. As the market's din enveloped them once more, few would guess that the transaction had been anything out of the ordinary.

"Thank you, my friend," Nicolas offered, allowing

himself a small smile. It was, after all, part of the game—
the give and take, the decorum of the hunt.

"Wish you luck with the sale," Henri called after him,
a wry edge to his voice.

Luck has its place in the antique trade, but so does
a discerning eye, Nicolas thought as he made his way
through the throng of the marketplace, the parcel tucked
securely under his arm.

*

"Nice lunch?" Isabella's voice floated from the back
room, tinged with the brightness of youth and
curiosity. She emerged, wiping her hands on a
cloth, her gaze settling on Nicolas' brown-paper parcel.
"Found anything interesting?"

"Perhaps," Nicolas replied, setting the package on the
counter with care as though it cradled more than just an
unremarkable painting. His eyes met Isabella's, a glint of
mischief alive within their blue depths.

Isabella leaned in, her eyes scanning the dull facade of
the painting before resting on the frame. "You think there
is any worth in this thing?" Her tone held scepticism,
yet she knew better than to question Nicolas' instincts.

"It's not what's on the canvas that intrigues, but rather
what encases it. The frame can be worth a couple hundred
if my hunch is correct." He lifted the frame, fingers
grazing over the ornate motifs carved into the wood.
"Sometimes value lies hidden beneath layers of neglect."

"Hundreds?" Isabella echoed, her earlier doubt giving way to admiration. "Then you have quite the eye, Nicolas."

"Let's work on it in the back room," he murmured, his thoughts turning inward as he contemplated the potential significance of his find.

Before doing anything with the painting, Nicolas has Isabella snap a few photos of the piece with her mobile. Then, with precise movements, Nicolas began to work on the frame, his tools selected with the expertise of a man well-versed in the delicate dance between art and its preservation. As he laboured, his mind wove through the tapestry of possibilities. Each brushstroke beneath his fingertips whispered secrets of its creation and journey.

The keen art history student Isabella watched with a curious and eager eye. She observed Nicolas's every move, learning from his skilled hands that treated every artefact with respect and reverence. The frame, with its intricate carvings and aged patina, hinted at stories untold, histories nestled in each swirl and curve.

As Nicolas gently cleaned the frame, revealing more of its former glory, Isabella's attention was drawn to the discarded canvas. At first glance, it was nothing more than an amateur's attempt at a fourteenth-century style landscape painting, unmarked by the flourish of a master's hand. However, her training had taught her to look beyond the obvious and seek the whispers of history in every thread of canvas.

With a furrowed brow, Isabella peered closer. There

was something peculiar, a shadow of something hidden beneath the layers of paint.

"Nicolas," she called out, her voice a mix of curiosity and excitement. "I think there's something underneath this painting."

Nicolas, his interest piqued, abandoned the frame and joined Isabella. Together, they examined the canvas, their eyes tracing the faint outlines barely visible under the existing image.

"You might be right, Isabella. This could be a pentimento," Nicolas mused, the term referring to an alteration in a painting that reveals the artist's change of mind.

Their curiosity now turned into a shared mission. They carefully began the process of uncovering the hidden painting. It was a delicate task, demanding patience and a steady hand.

"Be careful," Isabella cautioned from a respectful distance, her voice a soft melody against the quiet concentration.

Amidst the scent of old wood and varnish, Nicolas began removing the outer layers; a sense of suspense hung in the air. Each careful stroke peeled away years, revealing glimpses of a hidden world beneath. The outer paint, coarse and unrefined, gradually gave way under his expert hands, like mist dissipating to unveil a forgotten city.

Isabella watched with bated breath, her eyes reflecting the excitement of an art history student on the cusp of a potentially groundbreaking discovery. Nicolas's movements were precise, a dance of preservation and discovery, his tools gently coaxing the past into the present.

Slowly, as more of the original painting came into view, vibrant colours began to emerge from the canvas's depths. Unlike the dull hues of the outer layer, these were rich and lively, suggesting the work of a master's hand. Nicolas paused, his heart quickening. This was no amateur's work; it was something far more significant.

The emerging image was an interior scene, two men engaged in deep conversation, maybe negotiating. One man upright and noble, the other dignified despite the trials of hardship. But it was the wooden leg that caught Nicolas's eye, a distinctive feature that lent the portrait a powerful aura. Who was this man? A soldier? A pirate? A nobleman? The possibilities raced through Nicolas's mind.

With each layer removed, the portrait became more vivid, the man's expression more pronounced. He seemed to gaze out from the canvas, his eyes holding stories of a life steeped in adventure and, perhaps, tragedy. The wooden leg was rendered with such detail that it seemed almost real, a testament to the artist's skill and attention to detail.

Isabella leaned in closer, her fascination evident.

"Could this be the work of a master painter?" she whispered, almost afraid to disturb the solemnity of the moment. "The style is definitely seventeenth century…"

Nicolas did not answer immediately. His focus was entirely on the painting, on the mystery unfolding before him. Finally, the last of the outer paint was removed, and the portrait was revealed. The man with the wooden leg, captured in vibrant colours, seemed almost alive, his story etched into every line and shade. Nicolas stepped back, his eyes scanning the newly uncovered masterpiece.

"This," he said, his voice tinged with awe, "is a remarkable find."

The painting was a window into another era, a silent witness to the life of a man who had long been forgotten by history.

In the quiet of his shop, surrounded by relics of the past, Nicolas De Wever had uncovered a piece of history. The painting was more than just a canvas and paint; it was a mystery, a riddle from the past, waiting for someone like him to unravel its secrets.

*

Nicolas, nestled in the modest kitchen of his flat above the antique shop, was engaged in a culinary endeavour that mirrored the simplicity of his life. The kitchen, with its well-worn countertops and an array of pots and pans that had seen better days, was a stark contrast to the treasures that lay just a floor below. Tonight, he was preparing a two-course meal, which generally brought him a quiet joy, but his mind was elsewhere, lost in the enigma of the mysterious painting.

The first course was a classic Belgian leek soup. Nicolas

methodically chopped the leeks, their fresh, earthy scent mingling with the aroma of butter melting in the pot. He had always found comfort in the rhythm of cooking, the systematic process that, like restoring antiques, required patience and attention. But tonight, his thoughts drifted to the portrait hidden beneath layers of paint – a man with a wooden leg, a visage from a bygone era that beckoned with untold stories.

As the leeks sautéed, turning a gentle golden, Nicolas pondered over the painting's origins. Who was the one-legged man talking to, and why? Was this a painting depicting a historic event or merely the subject of an artist's creative whim? His mind wove tales of battles and bravery, of loss and triumph, each scenario more colourful than the last.

Distracted, Nicolas reached for the chicken stock, but in his preoccupation, he accidentally grabbed the beef stock instead. It was only when he poured it into the pot that he realised his mistake. The rich, dark liquid swirled into the sautéing leeks, tainting the soup with an unintended flavour. He sighed, a rare frown creasing his forehead. Much like his work with antiques, cooking demanded a presence of mind that he seemed to lack this evening.

Shaking his head, he turned his attention to the second course – a simple yet classic Belgian dish, stoofvlees, a slow-cooked beef stew. The preparation was straightforward, but it required time or a pressure cooker, which Nicolas preferred, something that mirrored his approach to unravelling the mysteries of the past.

Nicolas's thoughts returned to the painting as the stew simmered, its hearty aroma filling the small kitchen. The curiosity was unbearable. He needed answers and insights from someone more knowledgeable in the realm of art history.

Finally, with the stew gently bubbling on the stove and the leek soup, albeit altered, ready to be served, Nicolas made a decision. He wiped his hands on a kitchen towel, picked up the phone, and found the number he wanted.

"Dirk Meijer, please," he said when the call was answered. Dirk was a renowned art historian whose life was dedicated to uncovering and preserving the stories embedded in paint and canvas. If anyone could shed light on the mystery of the painting, it was him.

"Nicolas? What can I do for you?" came Dirk's familiar voice, a hint of curiosity in his tone.

Nicolas glanced at the simmering stew, then back at the phone. "Dirk, I have come across something extraordinary," he began his voice a mix of excitement and apprehension. "A painting that I believe hides a significant piece of history. I need your expertise."

On the other end of the line, Dirk's interest was piqued. "I'm intrigued, Nicolas. Tell me more."

As Nicolas recounted his discovery, the painting hidden beneath an amateur landscape, the man with the wooden leg emerging from the past, he felt a renewed sense of purpose. The soup's mishap forgotten he was now

embarking on a journey that bridged his two passions –
antiques and history – a journey that promised to unravel
a story waiting to be told.

3

The golden afternoon sunlight filtered through the tall, mullioned windows of Nicolas De Wever's shop, casting a warm glow over the curated selection of fine art and antiques. The day had been long – long and lonely. Isabella had a day off to study, and Nicolas had not done much more than wait for this moment.

Dirk Meijer was a man of quiet and scholarly grace, steeped in the knowledge of fine art and antiques; his reverence for history and craftsmanship was evident in the careful way he observed the details of the ornate Louis XV commode before him.

"The marquetry is exquisite," he commented, his stooped silhouette outlined by the gentle light.

Standing tall and poised beside an eighteenth-century tapestry, Nicolas allowed himself a modest smile. "Your approval means a great deal, Dirk. There are few with an eye as discerning as yours."

"Indeed," Dirk replied, adjusting his glasses with a practised gesture. "But your collection never disappoints." The faintest twinkle in his eyes betrayed his pleasure.

The shop was Nicolas' world, each item carefully chosen, every painting steeped in silent stories. It was a space that reflected his character—reserved yet rich with hidden depths. A Persian rug underfoot softened their steps as they moved past displays of Chinese porcelain to reach the back room where Nicolas had kept the painting.

"Is this the rumoured Vermeer?" Dirk asked, peering intently at the small canvas.

"Rumoured? I don't know about that," Nicolas teased, the corner of his mouth lifting just so. "I trust you'll tell me?"

Dirk chuckled—a low, rumbling sound that seemed to dance around the high ceilings. "Give me time, my friend. Give me time."

As Dirk immersed himself in studying the brushstrokes, Nicolas's thoughts drifted to the provenance of the painting, the delicate dance of authentication. He prided himself on not just the aesthetic beauty of the pieces but the histories they carried. His gallery was more than a mere shop; it was a gateway to the past.

"Nicolas," Dirk began, his voice laced with anticipation, "there's something about the light... It's ethereal."

"Vermeer's trademark," Nicolas replied, watching Dirk's reflection in the glass of a display case.

"I need more light, more space," Dirk said, waving his arms about. "It is no easy task to determine the authenticity of a masterpiece long thought lost to time."

Together, they moved the easel and the painting to the outer room, and there was a low growl from Dirk's stomach as he replaced the canvas.

"Let us ponder over something to eat," Dirk suggested, reluctantly turning away from the painting.

"An excellent idea," Nicolas replied. His heart

thrummed with the prospect of the evening ahead, a symphony of intellectual discourse and gourmet cuisine awaiting them. "I will fetch something from the bistro."

Nicolas's fingers traced the ornate handle of the shop's front door, an action mingled with a ceremonial sense of parting. "I'll just be a moment," he assured Dirk, whose eyes lingered on the veiled masterpiece with scholarly possessiveness. "Lock the door from within."

"Take your time," Dirk responded absently, barely glancing up from the painting. "The anticipation will only make the meal more enjoyable."

With a silent nod, Nicolas stepped out into the crisp evening air, leaving behind the hushed reverence that clung to the artefacts and canvases like a sacred mist. The soft click of the lock as the door closed behind him seemed unusually final, echoing slightly off the cobblestones of the quiet street.

His thoughts, however, remained inside, fluttering about like moths eager for the light of discovery. What secrets does the canvas hold? And what would Dirk uncover in his absence? He pondered these questions as his feet carried him toward the bistro around the corner, known for its delicate coq au vin and robust Bordeaux.

Could it really be genuine—a lost treasure unveiled at last? The prospect sent a shiver down his spine, not entirely from the chill of the evening. "To think, after all these years, to stumble upon such a find…" The idea was as intoxicating as the fine wine they would soon share.

Nicolas returned, arms laden with aromatic delights

from the bistro, his mind already salivating over the potential breakthroughs their conversation might yield.

The street was empty and unusually dark as he returned to the shop not more than thirty minutes later.

He knocked on the door. No answer. No movements inside. He pressed down the handle. Locked. Still locked, and as he peeked inside, he could see that the key was still in the keyhole.

He knocked again harder, expecting the distracted art historian to come and greet him. Silence answered instead. His knocks grew more insistent, the silence morphing into an ominous echo in the narrow street. A sense of dread crept over him. This was not the regular order of things; something was wrong. His heart raced as he considered his next move.

"Dirk?" Nicolas called out as he continued to knock. Only silence answered him, a silence that pressed heavily against his ears. He set the food down, a sense of dread clawing at his chest.

"Dirk, this isn't amusing," he said louder, annoyance feigning away the worry gnawing at his thoughts. No response came, only the sombre gaze of the centuries-old sculptures that lined the window.

The silence that enveloped Nicolas as he stood outside his shop was almost tangible, a heavy cloak that seemed to press down upon him. With no response to his knocking, a growing sense of alarm took hold. Peering through the door's glass pane, he scanned the familiar interior, a realm of antiquities that had always been a haven of peace and history. But today, something sinister lurked within its walls.

His eyes adjusted to the dim light filtering through the dusty windows, casting long, eerie shadows across the floor. At first, everything appeared as he had left it until his gaze settled on a dark, shadowy corner of the shop. There was something there, an anomaly amidst the orderliness.

As he intensified his gaze, a chilling realisation dawned on him. Lying in that darkened nook was a shape, a form that was grotesquely out of place amidst the ancient relics. It was a body resting in a pool of crimson that seemed to spread like a macabre inkblot on the old wooden floor.

Nicolas's breath caught in his throat, his heart pounding with fear and disbelief. The blood, dark and thick, was hardly visible against the shop's dark floorboards.

For a moment, time seemed to stand still; the shop transformed into a tableau of terror. Nicolas's mind raced, grappling with the horrifying sight before him.

"Mon Dieu..." The words tumbled from his mouth, a whisper lost amidst the chaos of his thoughts. He backed off abruptly, a surge of panic propelling him back. His eyes darted to the streets around him.

"Help! Someone help!" he shouted, though he knew no one would hear.

*

The wail of the sirens crescendoed into silence as the police vehicles lined the cobbled street outside Nicolas' shop. The flashing blue lights cast a spectral dance upon the meticulous brickwork of the surrounding buildings, each flash reflecting off the polished window panes and ricocheting through the refined space within.

Inspector Léonie Martens stepped out of her car with an air of quiet authority that seemed to command the scene before her. She was the picture of practicality; her short, curly blonde hair tousled just so, her piercing green eyes scanning the premises with analytical precision. A navy blazer hugged her athletic frame, the fabric taut across her shoulders as she moved. Her demeanour was calm, yet her presence was as sharp as the creases in her dark trousers.

"Inspector Martens," one of the officers greeted her, snapping a salute.

"Report," she said briefly, her voice betraying none of the emotion the scene before her might elicit in a less seasoned professional.

"Victim's name is Dirk Meijer, a renowned art historian. And this," he gestured towards Nicolas, "is the shop's owner, Nicolas De Wever."

Nicolas stood motionless, a sentinel amid the turmoil that had overtaken his sanctuary. The muted clink of forensic tools punctuated the silence, an affront to the shop's usual hush reserved for contemplation, not investigation. He felt a dissonance within him, as if he were a spectator in his own life, watching the scene unfold with detached horror.

"Mr. De Wever, can you tell me what happened?" Inspector Martens asked, her gaze locking onto his.

"I... I left to get us some food," Nicolas stammered, his voice barely above a whisper. "When I returned, the door was still locked from inside... but Dirk—he was..." His throat tightened around the words he couldn't bring himself to say.

"Dead," completed Martens softly, not unkindly, as she took in the sight of Dirk's body sprawled inelegantly on the polished wood floor.

"Why was Mr Meijer here?" she continued, her gaze returned to Nicolas.

"I bought a painting… He was examining a painting…" Nicolas explained, shaking his head slowly from side to side.

"And this painting, where is it now?" her eyes flicking to the barren easel.

"Vanished," Nicolas uttered, feeling the weight of suspicion settling upon him like dust on untouched antiques. "I don't understand. It was here, and everything was locked up tight."

"Locked, you say?" Martens mused aloud, a hand resting on her chin as she surveyed the room. "That suggests someone with access..."

Nicolas felt a surge of protest rise within him. The air in the gallery, once redolent with the subtle mix of aged canvas and beeswax polish, was now tainted by a sterile tang that clung to Nicolas De Wever's nostrils. He watched a forensics officer in crisp white overalls deftly navigate through the backroom—a sanctum where only the most discerning eyes were typically allowed. The officer's white gloves, as stark against the dark antique wood as a smear on a masterpiece, picked up flaxen fibres from the carpet, placed them into small plastic bags, and labelled them with meticulous care.

"Careful with the Géricault piece," Nicolas said, his voice a low murmur, noticing the officer inch too close to an unrestored painting propped against the wall.

"Everything will be handled with utmost respect, Mr. De Wever," Inspector Léonie Martens assured him, her gaze steady and piercing as she observed the process. "We need to gather every speck; it might lead to your friend's killer."

Nicolas nodded, swallowing the bitter taste of grief. Dirk Meijer had been more than a colleague; he'd been a beacon in the murky waters of art history and now, extinguished too soon, left behind a void no amount of scrutiny could fill.

A forensics officer in white baggy overalls and cap that made it impossible to determine if it was a man or a woman pushed past him carrying a pile of files and his laptop.

"We have to go through everything," said Inspector Martens calmly as he tried to protest. "Everything must be processed. Do you have a surveillance camera, Mr. De Wever?"

Nicolas shook his head.

"We'll need to take you down to the station for further questioning," Martens stated, her tone leaving no room for argument.

As he was escorted through the crowd of uniforms, past the forensics officer meticulously collecting evidence, Nicolas' heart hammered against his ribs. The gallery, his sanctuary of culture and history, had become a stage for tragedy, and he—despite his innocence—was a suspect in a drama he wished he could rewrite.

"Nicolas!" The familiar voice of Claire Dubois called out from the crowd as they approached the car. "Nice to see some decent police work," she teased. "They came back when they realised you sell such cheap antiquities."

He could hear her taunt and imagined the grin on her thin, red lips, but this was no time for humour. Nicolas did not even look up.

*

Nicolas was not made for police stations; he was accustomed to the soft light from a brass lamp and the soft cushion on an eighteenth-century chair. Yet here he sat on a cold metal chair under the harsh lights of the interrogation room. Inspector Léonie Martens paced before him, her steps measured, her green eyes flickering with the cogitation of a mind that missed nothing.

"Mr. De Wever," she began, her voice even, "you must understand the gravity of the situation. A man is dead in your gallery, a valuable painting is missing, and you are the last person known to have seen both."

"I do understand, Inspector," Nicolas replied, his voice steady despite the tremor of nerves beneath his skin. "But I assure you, my only concern was to share a meal with an old friend. I am as baffled by this tragedy as you are."

Martens leaned against the table, her gaze locked onto his. "That may be so. But I need more than your assurances; I need facts, clues... something to lead us away from this dead end. Who was with you in the shop today?"

Nicolas inhaled deeply, mentally sifting through the day's events. "It was a typical day, initially. My assistant, Isabella, was at her university classes, so I was alone at the shop."

He hesitated for a moment before continuing. "Only one customer came in today – a young woman who's been collecting pieces for a law firm. She wanted to know if I had any new items and picked up a few more for the firm and left. It was all quite routine."

Inspector Martens noted this and asked, "What happened after the customer left?"

"I spent most of the day waiting for the art historian, Dirk Meijer," Nicolas explained. "I've discovered something unusual in a painting and needed his opinion."

Intrigued, Martens leaned in. "What's unusual about this painting?"

Nicolas described how he had found a seemingly ordinary painting, but upon cleaning it, he uncovered another much older painting hidden beneath – an extraordinary piece depicting a man with a wooden leg.

"Do you think this painting is connected to what happened at your shop?" Martens inquired.

"I'm not sure," Nicolas admitted. "But the painting is extraordinary. I called Dirk Meijer for his expertise."

Martens queried further about the woman and other potential visitors, but Nicolas could offer no additional insights.

As the interview was wrapping up, Martens asked one more question. "This painting with the hidden image – did you document it in any way?"

That question triggered a realisation in Nicolas. "Yes, my assistant, Isabella, took a few photos of it with her mobile phone. She was fascinated by the discovery."

Martens's eyes lit up with interest. "We'll need those photographs, Mr. De Wever. They could be crucial to our investigation."

"Of course," Nicolas agreed, feeling a flicker of hope. Perhaps those photos held the key to understanding the day's horrifying events.

As the interrogation continued, Léonie Martens's focus shifted, her questions sharpening like the blade of a well-honed knife. "Let's discuss the nature of the crime, Mr. De Wever. We're dealing with what appears to be a locked-room murder. Are there any other entrances to your shop or the flat above it?"

Nicolas shook his head, his brow furrowing in thought. "No, there's only the front door. I always ensure it's locked when I leave. And there are no other ways in, to my knowledge."

The inspector pressed on, her gaze unyielding. "So, can you explain how someone could have entered and left under these circumstances?"

A sense of helplessness washed over Nicolas. "I can't explain it," he admitted, his voice tinged with frustration. "It doesn't make any sense."

Martens leaned back, her expression contemplative. "Could it have been a suicide?"

Nicolas felt a chill at the suggestion. "I don't see how. Dirk was killed with a knife. It's hard to imagine it as a suicide."

"The weapon," Martens said, shifting gears, "was it yours?"

Nicolas's heart skipped a beat. "Yes, that's from my collection; it's a ceremonial dagger from Southeast Asia. But I assure you, I had no part in this. That dagger was a part of my inventory, like many other items in the shop."

The room seemed to close in on him as the weight of the situation bore down. Nicolas, a man of antiques and history, found himself entangled in a present-day mystery far beyond his comprehension. The inspector's questions, though necessary, felt like an unwelcome intrusion into a world where he once felt in control.

Martens nodded, jotting down notes. "We'll need to take a closer look at your inventory and security measures. This appears to be a complex case."

As the interview concluded, Nicolas felt a mixture

of relief and unease. The questions raised by Inspector Martens lingered in his mind, each one a reminder of the enigmatic puzzle that his life had suddenly become.

"Thank you for your cooperation," Martens said as she closed her notebook. "We'll be in touch for further inquiries. In the meantime, please make arrangements to stay elsewhere. The shop needs to be thoroughly examined."

Stepping out of the police station, the evening air did little to dispel the fog of uncertainty that clouded his thoughts. The locked room murder, the mysterious painting, and now the implicating dagger from his own collection - all these elements wove a complex tapestry that seemed to have ensnared him in its threads.

4

Nicolas De Wever stirred from his slumber, the unfamiliar hum of the hotel air conditioner pulling him into a reluctant state of awareness. The plushness of the bed beneath him was a stark contrast to the modest mattress in his small flat above his beloved shop. He blinked against the sting of daylight that peeked through heavy drapes, painting soft golden streaks across the room's opulent decor. Squinting, he reached for his watch on the nightstand—its hands indicating it was well past his usual hour of rising.

"Damn it," he muttered under his breath as he swung his legs over the edge of the bed, feeling the carpet's lush fibres between his toes. He was a man displaced, an antique dealer without his shop, a man locked out of his home.

His suit, a sartorial comfort, hung over the armchair—a silent reminder of yesterday's upheaval. The police tape would still be crisscrossing the entrance to his apartment and shop, sealing away not just antiques and fine art but pieces of himself.

With a sigh, he picked up the phone, its weight familiar yet alien. Dialling with precision, he listened to the beep and trill until Isabella's voice crackled through the speaker.

"Isabella, it's Nicolas."

"Mr. De Wever!" she exclaimed, her tone a mix of surprise and concern. "I heard about what happened. Are you alright?"

"Quite so," he replied, though his furrowed brow betrayed his vexation. "Listen closely. You'll not be able to come to the shop today. But I need those photos of the painting—you know, the one Dirk was so engrossed with before... before everything transpired."

"Of course," Isabella answered, a hint of eagerness to assist weaving through her words. "I transferred them to your laptop right after I took them. They should be in the folder marked 'Urgent Appraisals.'"

"Ah, splendid work," Nicolas said, allowing a modicum of relief to seep into his voice. Yet even as he spoke, he realised his laptop was not with him, now evidence in some sterile police precinct, gnawed at him like a persistent itch.

"Thank you, Isabella. That will be all for now." He set the receiver down gently, his mind already plotting the retrieval of the digital keys to this mystery.

He stood and paced the confines of the room, each step a measured cadence as he replayed the previous day's events. The painting had been a beacon, luring Dirk Meijer towards knowledge—or perhaps peril. And now, Nicolas was left to navigate the shadowy waters of a case that seemed to stretch far beyond the canvas.

"Time and tide wait for no man," he whispered, a mantra to steel his resolve as he dressed methodically, ready to reclaim what was his and unravel the threads of a story woven through the very fabric of Belgian history.

Nicolas hovered over his breakfast, a modest array of croissants and fruit accompanied by strong coffee that competed with the dull throbbing in his head. The gentle clink of china and the soft murmur of conversation from other guests formed a symphony of morning routine within the hotel's dining room. Yet, Nicolas felt anything but routine.

"Mr. De Wever?" The question sliced through the humdrum noise, as crisp and clear as the sunlight streaming through the tall windows.

He looked up to find Inspector Léonie Martens standing before him—a figure of intent wrapped in professional garb. Her green eyes were sharp, her posture suggesting she was ready to chase down the truth as if it were a fugitive on the run.

"Inspector Martens," he replied, rising politely. "Please, join me."

She seated herself gracefully. The chair seemed almost too fragile for the weight of purpose she carried.

Léonie, sipping her coffee, began in a measured tone.

"Let's go over the facts again, Nicolas. You found the gallery locked from inside, with Dirk Meijer murdered and the painting gone. Can you think of any other way someone could have entered or left the shop?"

Absentmindedly putting pieces of fruit between his lips, Nicolas shook his head. "No, Inspector. There's only the front door: no back exit, no secret passages. I'm as baffled as you are. The door was locked from the inside, and the key was still in the keyhole."

"And the painting, the one you discovered, had another beneath it – it was missing from the scene?"

Nicolas nodded, a frown creasing his brow. "As your officer forced their way inside, the easel was empty, the painting gone. That painting..."

Léonie leaned forward, her eyes sharp. "Do you suspect anyone who might have been interested in it?"

Nicolas sighed, his mind racing with possibilities. "The painting's revelation of a historical figure from the revolution attracted quite a bit of attention. But I can't pinpoint anyone specific. It's not just an artwork; it's a piece of history. Anyone interested in that era's art could be a suspect."

Léonie took a thoughtful bite of a croissant. "What about the art historian Dirk Meijer? Did he mention anything unusual about the painting or show any signs of concern?"

"Dirk was excited, intrigued by its historical significance. He didn't express any fear or suspicion," Nicolas replied, his expression clouded with confusion. "He was supposed to help me uncover its secrets, not end up a victim in my own shop."

Martens leaned back, her expression contemplative. "And the murder weapon?"

"A ceremonial dagger from my collection," Nicolas admitted, his voice tinged with disbelief. "I never imagined it would be used for something so heinous."

The inspector sipped her coffee, mulling over the information. "We're dealing with a clever criminal, Mr. De Wever. Rest assured, we'll unravel this painting's mystery."

"Understanding art is not like solving equations," Nicolas began, his voice carrying the timbre of aged wood, "It requires... a sensitivity to the unspoken."

"Perhaps," Léonie replied, her words clipped like a sculptor's chisel, "but criminals aren't known for their subtlety. They leave traces as clear as a painter's signature."

Nicolas offered a thin smile that didn't quite reach his eyes. "And yet, without my laptop, those 'traces' remain hidden."

"Your laptop?" Léonie queried, an eyebrow arching in surprise. "What about your laptop, Mr. De Wever?"

"You took it," he murmured, his gaze drifting towards the window where the morning had begun to assert itself with more confidence. "The police confiscated it last night."

The tension between them stretched, taut as a fresh canvas on a frame. Léonie's practicality clashed with Nicolas's meticulous nature, each approach a different palette from which they were expected to paint a coherent picture.

"Was it collected from your shop?" The inspector's tone took on a sharper edge.

"Indeed, it was," he confirmed, his mind replaying the image of the forensic technician carrying away his belongings. His chest tightened at the thought of his world being sifted through by indifferent hands.

"Then I'll see it returned to you," Léonie assured him, though her certainty seemed to falter for the first time as if she, too, sensed the incongruence in the situation.

"Appreciated," Nicolas acknowledged dryly, the reality of his predicament settling upon him like dust on neglected silverware. He needed those photos, yet the idea of the authorities poring over his research was akin to strangers thumbing through a private journal.

"Once we have the photos, we can start piecing together the narrative," Léonie stated, standing now, her silhouette framed against the burgeoning day. "The painting will speak to us of its past and secrets."

"Assuming the past is willing to relinquish its grip," Nicolas countered, rising to meet her, his movements deliberate and measured. They both knew the obstacles ahead, the resistance of a mystery unwilling to be unravelled.

"Then we must be more persistent than history itself," Léonie declared, a detective's resolve steely in her voice.

"Are we now partners in this escapade?" His tone was dry.

"Seems so," she accepted, her voice betraying no hint of excitement or dread.

The partnership was uneasy, their methods discordant, but the pursuit of truth had a way of bridging even the most disparate minds. With the ghost of the missing laptop hanging between them, they moved toward the day, their quest for answers as insatiable as the thirst for knowledge itself.

*

The morning had matured into a crisp, golden haze by the time Nicolas De Wever and Inspector Léonie Martens arrived at the police station. The building, an austere edifice of grey stone, squatted amidst the grandeur of Brussels' architecture like an interloper, unapologetic in its utilitarian blandness.

"Inspector Martens," greeted the desk sergeant, his voice betraying a hint of wariness upon recognising her. "And this would be…?"

"Nicolas De Wever," Léonie introduced briskly, dispensing with pleasantries. "We're here to inquire about a laptop taken into custody from his shop."

"Ah," the sergeant murmured, fingers tapping across the keyboard with hesitant strokes. Nicolas stood beside Léonie, arms folded, studying the array of wanted posters smudging the walls like blots of guilt.

"Nothing has been logged here," the sergeant finally declared, brows furrowed.

"Impossible," Nicolas objected, his tone even but firm. "I saw one of the forensic technicians—short, slim—remove it along with a pile of documents from my inner room."

"Well, maybe they haven't had time to register it yet," the officer suggested, his gaze shifting uncomfortably between the two visitors.

Nicolas's mind raced, piecing together fragments of memory—the weight of the technician's gait as he carried the laptop, the careful way he balanced the stack of folders. It was all too vivid to be a trick of perception—a sense of foreboding coiled within him, whispering that this was no mere oversight.

"Perhaps there's been a misunderstanding," Nicolas suggested after a stretch of silence, his voice tinged with frustration. "But I assure you, the laptop is crucial."

"Mr. De Wever, I understand, but without a record..." the sergeant trailed off, helpless.

Léonie's hand rested briefly on Nicolas's arm—a silent counsel for calm. Her eyes, however, were flints sparking with determination. "Then consider this an official request to search the evidence room," Léonie interjected, her words clipped and authoritative.

"Inspector, you know I can't authorise that." The sergeant's plea was a mix of frustration and protocol.

"Then get someone who can," Léonie shot back, her eyes never leaving the man's face.

The impasse stretched taut between them, a mute standoff where the spoken word had capitulated to the will of those waiting for action.

Nicolas's mind revisited the tableau of his ransacked shop, the vacant space where his laptop once lay—a void now mirrored by the empty-handedness of the law. The realisation dawned upon him, cold and stark, that their quest for truth had become a navigation through shadows, where every light cast deeper darkness upon their path.

"There is another way," he said, facing Léonie. Her green eyes met his determined gaze as he moved away. "Can I borrow your phone?"

Nicolas's fingers danced over the keys of her phone with a sense of urgency that betrayed the calm facade he projected.

"Isabella," he spoke briskly when she answered, "my laptop is entangled in some bureaucratic snarl at the police station. I need you to forward the photos of the painting to Inspector Martens' email immediately."

"Of course, Nico," came the swift reply, her voice laced with concern but underscored by efficiency. "Consider it done."

"Thank you," he murmured as he ended the call. Nicolas caught Léonie Martens' gaze, noting the minute lift of her eyebrow—an indication of intrigue and impatience.

"Photos are on their way to you now," he informed her.

"Good," Léonie acknowledged with a nod, eyeing her device in anticipation.

Within moments, the chime of an incoming email pierced the hushed atmosphere. Léonie's eyes scanned the photographs, her expression sharpening. Nicolas leaned in, peering at the image of the man with a wooden leg receiving a book from a uniformed figure. The scene was depicted with such clarity that it seemed to leap from the digital confines, begging for interpretation.

"Look at the detail here," Nicolas pointed out, tapping

where the light fell on the wooden limb, highlighting the rough texture against the polished floorboards. "This is more than mere art; it's history captured in oil and canvas."

"The Napoleonic era, perhaps?" Léonie queried, her mind stitching together fragments of historical knowledge.

"Let's find out. Can I get access to a computer?" Nicolas replied.

They made their way to Léonie Martens's desk at the crime squad, and Nicolas embarked on a journey through cyberspace. He waded through digital archives and collections, casting nets to historians who might shed light upon the enigmatic figure with the prosthetic appendage.

"Anything?" Léonie's voice was tinged with anticipation. She leaned closer to the screen, her finger tracing the lines of the oil painting that now filled the expanse of their view. The depicted scene was a solemn exchange between two men—one proudly bearing the uniform of an early nineteenth-century soldier, the other, a figure of resilience with his wooden prosthetic leg.

"Patience," he replied, though his heart raced as much as hers. "Our wooden-legged friend is elusive but not beyond discovery."

As they waited, Léonie's gaze lingered on the painting. "There's a gravity to this transaction," she reflected aloud. "A book being passed with such ceremony—it must be significant."

"Indeed." Nicolas's thumb paused mid-scroll as a historian replied with genuine curiosity about their inquiry. The academic promised to delve into records posthaste, sensing the import of their quest.

"Someone will get back to us soon," he said, locking eyes with Léonie, who nodded, her earlier scepticism melting into a shared resolve.

"Until then, we wait," she concluded, but her foot tapped a silent rhythm beneath the table—a metronome to the urgency that had taken root within them both.

"Waiting," Nicolas mused internally, "is simply the quiet cousin of action." His thoughts were a whirling tapestry of speculation and theory—each thread pulling taut with the weight of potential revelation. The tension between stillness and the chase of discovery threaded through him, binding him to the enigma before them.

"Could it be Jean-Joseph Charlier?" he murmured, his voice a low hum in the silence of their anticipation. "Wasn't he called Jambe de Bois?"

Léonie's eyes sharpened, her analytical mind flicking through the pages of her mental dossier on prominent historical figures. "The Charlier family," she mused aloud. "Pascal Charlier has been very vocal about his lineage."

"Yes." Nicolas nodded, his thoughts knitting together fragments of information. "He's been using his ancestor's narrative to stoke the fires of nationalism—'Belgium First' is practically built on the legacy of the hero Jean-Joseph."

"Hero... or pawn?" Léonie's question hung in the

air, tinged with cynicism as she pondered the political machinations at play.

"Perhaps both," Nicolas shrugged.

"Maybe this is more than just art—it's a political statement, wrapped in a riddle, steeped in history," Nicolas spoke, his hands slicing the air as if to unravel the mystery physically.

"Then we need to understand not just the painting but also the book's relevance," Léonie said, her eyes alight with the thrill of the chase.

"Indeed," Nicolas echoed, pausing in his tracks. "We must delve deeper into the Charlier lineage. Understand the man, the myth, the message."

"Starting with Pascal," Léonie suggested her voice a mix of pragmatism and excitement.

"Starting with Pascal," Nicolas echoed, feeling the weight of history pressing upon their shoulders. The gravity of their discovery held them in a silent pact—an unspoken vow to excavate the truth buried in layers of paint and propaganda.

Nicolas leaned forward, his elbows resting on the Investigator's worn desk that bore the traces of frustrated police work and unsolved cases.

"An interview with Pascal Charlier seems imperative," he murmured, his gaze lost somewhere between the computer screen before him and the centuries-old intrigue they were unravelling. "His fervent use of his ancestor's image could be the linchpin in understanding the murder."

"Agreed," Léonie replied, sipping her coffee with measured calm. "But we must approach with caution. Pascal is not one to suffer prying eyes gladly, especially when his political ambitions are at stake."

The shrill signal from Martens's mobile interrupted their thoughts, and she answered with irritation evident to the caller. A few seconds later, a smile crossed her thin lips as she looked up at Nicolas.

"They are finished with the crime scene now. You can go home."

*

Nicolas De Wever stepped out of the police station, his footfalls echoing softly on the pavement. The brisk chill of the morning air had been replaced by a grey, damp wind that crept through his suit. He paused, allowing himself a moment to take in the frantic noise of the city.

"Inspector Martens," he addressed Léonie, who emerged beside him, her green eyes scanning the street with an alertness that seemed to miss nothing. "Our next move should be—"

"I will start with some discreet inquiries," she interjected smoothly, her voice low and composed. "You shall go home and rest. This is a job for the police now."

Nicolas nodded.

"But don't tell anyone about the photos, Nicolas. If the painting was worth killing for, so may the photos be."

5

As Nicolas pushed open the door to his antique shop, a wave of weariness washed over him. The chaos left behind by the police investigation seemed to mock him as he surveyed the disarray: paintings askew on the walls, artefacts placed haphazardly atop one another, and papers strewn about the floor like fallen leaves in autumn. He sighed, running a hand through his dark hair, streaked with silver strands that spoke of experience rather than age. Where does one even begin to restore order from this turmoil?

His blue eyes, sharp like a falcon's gaze, took in the damage with quiet determination. Despite the fatigue weighing down his slender frame, Nicolas knew that his haven of art and history must be returned to its former glory. With a deep breath, he rolled up his sleeves and began the process of meticulously tidying the space.

He lifted a displaced painting with great care. As if cradling a newborn, he carried the artwork to its rightful place on the wall, adjusting it until it hung just so—a testament to his keen eye for detail. In every movement, in every gentle touch, Nicolas displayed a reverence for the pieces he tended to; each item, whether an ancient sculpture or a delicate porcelain figurine, was treated with the utmost respect.

Hours slipped past as Nicolas moved throughout the

shop, straightening, rearranging, and restoring balance. The world outside ceased to exist as he focused on the task at hand, his mind a whirlwind of thoughts and memories evoked by the objects he handled. Each piece had a story to tell, and he was a willing listener.

The jade figurine from the Han dynasty seemed to whisper memories of its first encounter with Nicolas as he gently placed it on its shelf. He had found it in a dusty corner in Beijing, instantly recognizing its specialness. Under his attentive care, it now shone with renewed brilliance.

With the last paper neatly stacked, Nicolas took a moment to survey his shop. From dishevelled chaos, it had transformed into a sanctuary of art and history, a testament to his dedication and passion. He murmured to himself about the beauty in order, reflecting on how this philosophy, more than just an aesthetic choice, guided his life. Each artefact and artwork in its place of honour provided him solace, especially now, amid the turmoil following Dirk Meijer's murder and the ongoing investigation.

He walked over to the door, his movements reflecting a ritualistic dedication, and flipped the sign to 'Open'. The shop's quiet was a stark contrast to the chaotic events of the last few days.

His gaze fell upon the old frame, the very item that had unwittingly catapulted him into the heart of a mystery that seemed to deepen with each passing hour. The frame, once a mere holder of the now-stolen painting, had become a symbol of the unforeseen turmoil in his life. He picked it up, his fingers tracing over the intricate carvings, feeling the weight of history in his hands.

As he examined the frame, Nicolas couldn't help but reflect on the recent events. The murder in his shop, the involvement of the police, and the enigmatic painting that had vanished – it all seemed like a puzzle missing crucial pieces. The frame, an artefact of exquisite craftsmanship, was now a solitary remnant of a mystery that had been stripped from his grasp.

Turning the frame over in his hands, Nicolas's fingertips traced the ornate carvings, a relic from ages past that had been tucked away amidst the chaos. With each curve and line, he felt a sense of reverence for the skilled hands that had crafted it perhaps centuries ago. His blue eyes shimmered with curiosity as he explored its exquisite beauty, seeking solace in the intricate designs that whispered secrets of history.

"Such artistry," he murmured to himself, his fingers lingering on a particularly elaborate knot-work pattern. Then, he noticed something odd—a subtle indentation in the wood, carefully concealed by the adornments. His pulse quickened, and he felt a thrill of anticipation coursing through his veins.

"Could it be?" he wondered, his heart pounding as he gently pressed on the hidden cavity. To his delight, the panel gave way, revealing a secret compartment that lay nestled within the depths of the frame.

"Ah, mon Dieu," Nicolas breathed, his eyes widening in excitement. He had stumbled upon countless treasures in his time, but few matched the thrill of uncovering a clandestine hideaway such as this. The air around him seemed to hum with energy, as though the frame itself was urging him to explore its secrets further.

What could be concealed within? His mind racing with possibilities. Perhaps a message from the past or a fragment of history long since forgotten? As his fingers brushed against a small, folded piece of paper, he felt the weight of the moment settle upon him.

"Voilà," he whispered, carefully extracting the fragile parchment from its resting place. Unfolding it with the utmost care, he found himself gazing upon a cryptic note penned in an elegant script that seemed to dance across the page. It was a series of numbers.

The delicate note might have crumbled to dust if Nicolas's hands had not been so steady. He held his breath as though the very air around him could disintegrate the relic from a bygone era. The parchment possessed an ethereal quality, its surface mottled with age, yet the script retained a remarkable clarity. His eyes traced the inked curves and swirls, seeking meaning among the cryptic numbers.

"Curious," he murmured, the whisper barely escaping his lips. He regarded the note as though it were a sentient being, its message obscured by the passage of time.

The delicate chime of the doorbell resounded through Nicolas's shop, drawing him out of his reverie. He looked up from the cryptic note to see Léonie Martens standing before him with a determined expression that could only signify important information.

"Nicolas," she began breathlessly, her eyes alight with urgency, "I've come across something significant in our investigation."

"Ah, Inspector Martens," he replied, momentarily taken aback by her arrival. "Please, do come in and share your findings."

Léonie stepped further into the shop, her gaze sweeping over the carefully arranged artefacts and artworks as she approached Nicolas. Her hands clutched a small plastic evidence bag containing what appeared to be a bright yellow piece of plastic.

"During our examination of Dirk Meijer's body, we discovered this earring grasped tightly in his hand," she explained, holding the bag aloft for Nicolas to inspect more closely. "It seems to have been torn from someone's ear during the struggle."

Nicolas's heart gave an involuntary jolt as he recognized the flamboyant piece of jewellery. It immediately brought to mind the vivacious girl from the law firm who had visited his shop not long ago. The connection was undeniable.

"Good God!" he exclaimed, the implications of this discovery dawning on him like a cold, unwelcome sunrise. "This is the same earring worn by that ostentatious young woman from the law firm! What possible connection could she have to Dirk's murder?"

"Nicolas," Léonie interjected, her voice firm yet compassionate, "we mustn't jump to conclusions. This may be nothing more than a coincidence, albeit a striking one."

Nicolas, his mind racing with theories and speculations, paced the room restlessly.

"But think about it, Léonie," he urged, his voice tinged with intrigue and apprehension. "This young woman, she's been in and out of my shop several times, looking for something unique for the firm. Could it be possible that she was after this particular painting all along?"

He paused, considering the possibilities. "Or what if she's involved with a secret society? Could her interest in art be a facade for something more sinister? Perhaps she's acting on behalf of someone else, using her visits as a cover to keep an eye on the painting."

Léonie listened intently, her expression thoughtful. "It's a compelling line of thought, Nicolas, but we need solid evidence. Her being at your shop and owning a similar earring is circumstantial at best. We can't overlook other possibilities - maybe someone else planted the earring to mislead us."

Nicolas nodded, acknowledging her point. "You're right, we can't be hasty. But I can't shake off this feeling that there's more to her than meets the eye. What if she's a pawn in a larger game, unknowingly entangled in this mystery? Or worse, what if she's a key player, cleverly disguised behind her flamboyant attire and seemingly innocent demeanour?"

Léonie nodded, her eyes reflecting the seriousness of the situation. "We'll follow this lead, Nicolas. Let's gather more information about her and her visits to your shop. But remember, appearances can be deceiving in mysteries as tangled as this."

"Indeed, you are right," he conceded, his gaze letting go of the vibrant earring and meeting Léonie's. "I have also found something."

Nicolas reached for the old frame that had once cradled the now-stolen painting. With careful fingers, he opened the secret compartment hidden in its ornate carvings. "In here I found this," he said, handing the small note to Léonie.

Léonie unfolded the note, revealing a series of cryptic numbers arranged in an enigmatic sequence. "What could this mean?" she mused, her eyes scanning the digits.

Nicolas leaned in, his curiosity piqued. "At first, I thought it might be a date or coordinate. But I don't understand it. Could it be a code, a part of a larger puzzle?"

Léonie pondered, her brow furrowing in concentration. "It's not immediately clear. These numbers could represent anything – a specific location, a key to a cipher, or maybe even a reference to an event or an artwork. We should cross-reference them with historical records, see if there's any connection to this case at all."

Nicolas nodded in agreement. "It's a long shot, but perhaps this sequence is linked to the painting's hidden history. Maybe it's a clue left behind, meant to be uncovered and understood by someone in the future."

Together, they studied the cryptic message, aware that they were holding a piece of the puzzle, a fragment of a secret that had been concealed for centuries. The numbers, silent and inscrutable, held the potential to unlock another door in the labyrinthine mystery that had engulfed Nicolas's life.

The pale afternoon light filtering through the shop's windows gave the scene an air of solemnity. Nicolas and Léonie stood side by side, the bright yellow earring glinting between them like a beacon in the dimly lit room and by its side the pale old note with its cryptic numbers. Their expressions mirrored one another's, both equally committed and focused on the task at hand. It was clear that they would not rest until they had uncovered the truth behind Dirk Meijer's murder and the theft of the enigmatic painting.

"Nicolas," a voice resounded through the shop, causing them to startle. The young gallery assistant stood at a respectful distance, her expression a mixture of concern and curiosity. "Is everything all right?"

"Ah, Isabella," Nicolas replied, his voice tight with exhilaration. "This is Inspector Léonie Martens. She is leading the investigation."

Isabella approached them and greeted the Inspector.

Nicolas turned to Isabella, his young assistant, who scanned the shop for anything misplaced. "Isabella, have you seen the girl from the law firm around here more than once?" he asked, his voice laced with a subtle urgency.

Isabella paused, thinking. "No, I don't recall seeing her more than the few times she came to pick up items for the firm," she replied, her brow furrowing in concentration. "She always seemed straightforward, just here for business."

As they spoke, Isabella's eyes fell upon the old frame, its intricate carvings hinting at a hidden depth. Her keen eyes didn't miss the peculiar detail in the old frame as she meticulously arranged a display in Nicolas's shop.

"What's this?" she asked, her curiosity piqued by the frame's hidden compartment.

Nicolas, catching a discreet glance from Inspector Léonie Martens, quickly improvised.

"Ah, yes, I found that too. An interesting little compartment, but it was empty," he said, his voice casual but firm. He saw Isabella's curiosity linger, and to divert her attention, he pointed out the craftsmanship of the compartment. "Notice the intricacy with which this was constructed. It's a fine example of the skill and ingenuity of the period," he explained, guiding her focus to the artistic details rather than its contents.

Fascinated by the craftsmanship, Isabella nodded in agreement, her initial suspicion easing. Nicolas seized the opportunity to redirect the conversation.

"Could you keep an eye on the shop for a while? Inspector Martens and I must attend to some matters regarding this investigation."

"Of course, Nicolas," Isabella replied, her attention now entirely on the frame's artistic merit. As she delved into examining the frame, Nicolas and Léonie discreetly exited the shop, the weight of the hidden note and the unanswered questions pressing on their minds.

*

In a dimly lit corner of a quiet café, Nicolas De Wever and Inspector Léonie Martens sat huddled over their coffee, the weight of the unresolved mystery hanging heavily between them. Nicolas, with a furrowed brow, broke the silence.

"Léonie, what are our options? We have so little to go on – just the earring and this cryptic note."

Léonie, her gaze fixed on the note, replied thoughtfully, "We're at a crossroads, Nicolas. The earring could be a vital clue, pointing us towards the law firm. And this note," she gestured to the paper, "could unlock a part of this puzzle we haven't even considered yet. But first things first, we need to identify the woman from the law firm."

Nicolas nodded in agreement. "I know the address of the firm but not her name. She's a new customer, and our interactions were always strictly professional."

Léonie leaned back, her mind working through the possibilities. "Then that's where we start. We visit the law firm; someone there must know her. It's a starting point, at least."

Nicolas, though anxious, felt a surge of hope. He

trusted Léonie's experience and judgement. Her methodical approach had already shed light on aspects of the case he would have otherwise missed.

Resolved, they finished their coffee and prepared to leave. As they stepped out into the bustling streets of Brussels, Léonie's phone rang. Her team had a minor update, but nothing significantly advanced their case. The day was waning, and the urgency to act was palpable.

6

Upon reaching the law firm of Verhaegen & Delacroix, a modern building that stood in stark contrast to the aged beauty of Nicolas's shop, they were greeted by a receptionist. Léonie introduced herself and Nicolas, explaining their need to speak with someone in charge.

After a brief hesitation, the receptionist led them to a meeting room, where a senior partner soon joined them. Léonie explained the situation as delicately as possible, revealing the earring and asking if they recognised it or could identify the woman who frequented Nicolas's shop.

The law firm's senior partner, a tall man with a stern demeanour, greeted Inspector Léonie Martens and Nicolas De Wever with a cool politeness that quickly turned frosty as the purpose of their visit became evident. They found themselves seated in a stark, modern meeting room, a sharp contrast to the warmth of Nicolas's shop.

Léonie began cautiously, explaining their investigation and the mysterious earring. "This piece was found at a crime scene. We believe it may belong to one of your employees, who's been working on decorating your reception area."

The senior partner's expression hardened. "I must remind you that without a warrant, I am not obligated to disclose any information about our employees or, clients or other partners. This is a matter of privacy and confidentiality."

Nicolas, sensing the growing tension, interjected. "Most of the items for your new reception area came from my shop. We're just trying to understand if there's any connection..."

The partner cut him off sharply. "Mr. De Wever, while your concern is noted, I cannot breach our firm's policy based on speculation. You're asking for privileged information." He quoted legal paragraphs with practised ease, building a wall of legal jargon around them.

Léonie, frustrated but composed, pressed on. "We're merely trying to follow a lead. Any assistance you provide could be crucial to our investigation."

The partner leaned back in his chair, his gaze steely. "Unless you have concrete evidence implicating someone from this firm, I'm afraid I cannot help you." His tone suggested finality, an apparent dismissal of their queries.

As they left the meeting, the air between Nicolas and Léonie was thick with unsaid words. The partner's hostility and refusal to even name the decorator hinted at something more profound. This mystery extended beyond the confines of Nicolas's shop and the stolen painting.

"Something doesn't add up," Léonie murmured as they stepped out into the bustling street. "His defensiveness, it's almost as if he's protecting someone... or something."

Nicolas nodded, his mind racing with possibilities.

"Could the firm be involved in some way? Or is that just the way lawyers behave?"

"Nicolas, I fear that without a solid lead, we are simply chasing shadows," Léonie sighed, a hint of weariness creeping into her voice. Her piercing green eyes scanned the streets before them.

Nicolas's slender fingers tapped thoughtfully on the lapel of his jacket. "We must delve deeper – unearth new evidence that will untangle this web of mystery."

"Could it be that we've overlooked something?" Léonie pondered aloud. "Some vital clue hidden within the encrypted note?"

"Perchance," Nicolas mused, the spark of determination igniting in his sharp blue eyes. He retrieved the enigmatic message from his pocket and held it before them. "Let us scrutinise the note once more."

They found two vacant chairs at a street-side café, its quaint charm a brief respite from the escalating complexities of their investigation. They sat at a secluded table; the cryptic note spread before them with its string of numbers. A gentle breeze carried the murmurs of the city as they bent over the parchment. Léonie's analytical mind raced, seeking patterns and connections that had evaded them thus far. Nicolas, too, was consumed by the pursuit of truth, his keen eye for detail scanning the cryptic symbols and encoded words.

Nicolas's fingers traced the numbers. "Could these be coordinates?" he mused, the possibility hanging in the air like an unanswered question.

Léonie considered it, sipping her coffee thoughtfully. "It's plausible, but the sequence doesn't fit any standard coordinate system. And why would a seventeenth-century painting be linked to a specific location in this manner?"

Dismissing the idea, Nicolas ventured, "What about a secret society code? The painting's history might be entangled with some clandestine group."

Léonie nodded. "It's an intriguing thought. Secret societies often used cryptic means of communication. But without knowledge of their specific coding system, we're at a dead end."

Their conversation meandered through various theories - an encryption for a hidden message, a mathematical or scientific reference, even a biblical verse. Each hypothesis seemed to hit a wall, lacking the context or the key to unlock its meaning.

"The numbers must mean something," Nicolas said, frustration edging his voice. "What if it's a cipher or encryption?"

Léonie leaned forward, her eyes reflecting the spark of a new challenge. "Encryption in the 1800s... We're likely looking at something predating modern cryptographic methods. Think simpler, more foundational."

They delved into the history of cryptography, discussing the evolution of secret writing from ancient times to the nineteenth century. "Back then, common methods included substitution ciphers, where each letter or number is replaced with another," Léonie explained.

"Or transposition ciphers, where the order of the elements is rearranged."

Nicolas nodded, absorbing the information. "But without the key or the cipher itself, how do we decipher it?"

"That's the crux," Léonie said, her mind working through the puzzle. "We need to find a link, something that connects the painting or its history to a potential cipher."

Returning to the note, Nicolas proposed, "What if the key lies in the painting's history? Something from the artist's life or the era it was created in?"

Léonie's eyes lit up. "Yes, something contemporary with the painting's creation. We must dive deeper into that period, look into common encryption methods used at the time, cultural references, anything that could serve as a potential key."

Léonie, her brow knitted in concentration, paused in her examination of the note. She glanced at Nicolas, who was equally engrossed in the puzzle before them. "I just realised something," she began, her voice calm but insistent. "I must request a warrant to search the law firm. There may be more evidence hidden there – something we've missed."

"Indeed," Nicolas agreed, his eyes never leaving the parchment.

Léonie stood abruptly but did not leave the table. As she dialled the number for police chief Moreau, her posture exuded an air of authority and urgency.

"Chief Moreau?" she said crisply as the call connected. "This is Inspector Martens. I need a warrant to search the law firm of Verhaegen & Delacroix. I believe there may be pertinent evidence related to our investigation concealed within their premises."

Her words were met with a brief silence, followed by a gruff response from the chief.

"Very well, Inspector," Chief Moreau conceded. "But you'd best be right about this. We cannot afford any missteps in this case."

"Understood, sir," Léonie replied, her tone resolute. "Thank you." As she ended the call, her eyes met Nicolas', a fire of anticipation burning within them.

As Léonie sat down again, her words about searching for more evidence echoed in Nicolas' mind. He stared intently at the enigmatic symbols on the parchment, his thoughts racing, when suddenly, a memory surfaced like a bubble rising to the surface of still water.

"Of course!" he exclaimed, his eyes widening with realisation. "Henri! You remember that I told you about Henri, the man who sold me the painting at the market?"

"Sure," Léonie replied, furrowing her brow in an effort to recall the encounter.

"Perhaps Henri knows more about the painting's origins than we've given him credit for," Nicolas mused, his excitement palpable. "If we can find and persuade him to share what he knows, it may provide us with the lead we desperately need."

"Very well," Léonie agreed, her voice laced with

cautious optimism. "Then let us seek out Henri at once. With any luck, he will be able to shed light on the shadows that obscure our path."

The afternoon sun cast a warm glow upon the narrow streets of Brussels as Nicolas and Léonie made their way to the bustling market where he had last encountered Henri. The scent of aged flowers and fresh fruits mixed with wood and worn leather filled the air, mingling with the murmur of hushed negotiations and the delicate clinking of fine porcelain.

"Nicolas," Léonie whispered, her eyes scanning the stalls for a familiar face, "are you certain Henri will still be here? It has been quite some time since…"

"His stall is a fixture of this market," Nicolas cut her off, his gaze never wavering from the task at hand. "I have faith that we shall find him again."

As if fate itself were guiding them, they soon spotted the cheerful figure of Henri standing behind a table laden with items from a bygone era. He greeted them with a warm smile, seemingly oblivious to the gravity of their inquiry.

"Ah, Monsieur De Wever!" he exclaimed, extending a hand in greeting. "It has been too long since our last encounter. And who is this lovely lady?"

"Inspector Léonie Martens," she replied, returning his handshake firmly. "We have come to ask you about a painting you sold to Nicolas some days ago."

"Ah, yes," Henri said, his brow furrowing as he tried

to recall the transaction. "I sell so many paintings, you see. Can you describe it for me?"

"Of course," Nicolas replied, reaching into his pocket to retrieve his mobile and the photograph of the painting. "It was this one, depicting this rather bland landscape."

Henri's eyes widened as he studied the image, and a spark of recognition ignited within him. "Yes, I remember now! Such a stunning piece. I acquired it from an artist named Gaston Dupont."

"Tell us more about this Dupont," Léonie urged, her voice betraying her eagerness for information.

"Ah, Gaston," Henri mused, his eyes taking on a distant quality as he delved into his memories. "A most enigmatic figure, that one. He would frequent this market, selling his paintings at a fraction of their true worth, always in a hurry to be rid of them."

"Did you ever discuss the origins of this particular painting with him?" Nicolas asked, his fingers tracing the signature "G D" on the photograph.

"Only briefly," Henri replied, shaking his head as if to clear the cobwebs from his thoughts. "He mentioned something, but nothing of real importance. And I must admit, I was more interested in the profit to be made than in unravelling the mysteries of its creation."

"Indeed," Léonie murmured, exchanging a glance with Nicolas. It seemed they were drawing closer to the heart of the matter, each new revelation pulling back another veil to reveal a tantalising glimpse of the truth.

"Thank you, Henri," Nicolas said, his voice tinged with gratitude and determination.

"Think nothing of it, my friends," Henri replied, waving away their thanks with a jovial flourish. "I am simply glad to be of service."

As they turned to leave the market, Nicolas and Léonie felt that they had taken a significant step forward in their investigation. The enigmatic Gaston Dupont now loomed large in their minds, his potential involvement in both the creation of the painting and the sinister events surrounding it casting a long shadow over their path.

And yet, beneath the shroud of uncertainty, a flame of determination burned brightly within them. They would not rest until they had uncovered the truth, no matter the treacherous road ahead.

Their minds whirled with the revelation of Gaston Dupont's connection to the mysterious painting as they strolled back towards Nicolas' shop. The warmth of the afternoon's sun rays did little to dispel the chill that had settled in their bones as they contemplated the implications of Henri's recollections.

"Forgive me, Nicolas," Léonie began, her voice hesitant yet tinged with urgency. "But I cannot help but feel we have stumbled upon something far greater than we first imagined. Gaston Dupont is not merely a name in the art world; he has a certain...notoriety."

"Ah, you refer to his reputation as an art forger," Nicolas replied, his eyes narrowing as he considered this new information. "I must admit, I am familiar with the whispers that surround him."

"Indeed," Léonie continued, casting a furtive glance around them as if to ensure they were not overheard. "His skill in replicating the works of the Old Masters is said to be unparalleled. But what could this mean for the painting? And how does it connect to the law firm and the murder of Dirk Meijer? If at all?"

"An intriguing conundrum," Nicolas mused, his fingers tracing the outline of the encrypted note still nestled in his pocket. "Dupont's motives elude me, but one thing is clear: we must delve deeper into his world to make sense of this tangled web."

"Agreed," Léonie replied, nodding her determination. "In all my years as an inspector, I have never encountered a case quite like this one. We must tread carefully, Nicolas, for who knows what dangers we may encounter in our pursuit of the truth."

"Your caution is well-founded, Léonie," Nicolas acknowledged, his voice sombre. "And yet, I cannot help but feel we are on the cusp of a great discovery. The hunt for answers has become an irresistible lure, drawing me onward despite the potential perils that may lie in wait."

"I know the feeling," Léonie admitted, her eyes shimmering with resolve. "Mayhap Gaston Dupont holds the key to unlocking the secrets of the painting – and perhaps even to the machinations of the locked room mystery itself."

"Maybe," Nicolas murmured as they stopped before

the familiar facade of Nicolas' shop. Léonie looked at him, and they shared a determined glance, their minds alight with anticipation. The pursuit of truth would lead them down a treacherous path, but neither would rest until the mysteries surrounding the painting had been laid bare and justice had been served.

"Confronting Dupont will not be without risk," Léonie cautioned, her eyes fixed on the street. "His connections run deep within the art world's underbelly, and he has eluded capture on more than one occasion. You must be aware of this."

Nicolas nodded thoughtfully, his sharp blue eyes reflecting the soft light of the streetlamp. "I see, but I must learn what he knows about the painting and its provenance – and if he had any part in Meijer's untimely death."

"Agreed," Léonie replied, determination etched upon her face. "So, discretion will be our ally," she mused.

"Maybe we can approach him as potential clients seeking his expertise rather than as adversaries bent on exposing his misdeeds," Nicolas suggested.

Léonie paused, looking back at the darkened windows of the shop. "For now, let us gather our thoughts and plan our encounter with meticulous care."

*

Less than an hour later, Inspector Léonie Martens and Nicolas De Wever embarked on a new lead. Léonie had obtained Gaston Dupont's address from her colleagues in the police's art department, a potential key to unravelling the mystery of the stolen painting.

The address led them to a neglected part of the city, where the buildings bore the weight of age and neglect. They walked through narrow streets, their footsteps echoing in the eerie silence that hung over the area. Nicolas glanced around, noting the stark contrast to the vibrant bustle of his own neighbourhood.

As they approached Gaston Dupont's studio, a sense of trepidation settled over them. The studio was located in an old, decrepit building at the end of a dimly lit alley. Its facade was covered in peeling paint and graffiti, the windows grimy and opaque.

Léonie paused, surveying the building with a practised eye.

"This place has seen better days," she remarked, her voice low. "Let's proceed cautiously."

Nicolas nodded, his heart pounding with a mix of apprehension and anticipation. They made their way to the entrance, every creak of the old wooden steps amplifying their anxiety. The door to the studio was aged, its paint chipped and faded, a silent testament to the passage of time.

As they reached the door, Léonie reached for her badge, preparing to announce their presence. Nicolas stood beside her, his mind racing with possibilities of what they might find inside. Would Gaston Dupont provide the answers they sought, or would this be another dead end in their investigation?

Suddenly, the dim alleyway was bathed in a harsh, unexpected light. The studio's interior lights flickered on, casting a glow through the grimy windows and startling both Léonie and Nicolas. They froze, their eyes locked on the door that now seemed a gateway to untold secrets.

The sudden illumination of the studio felt ominous as if they were about to uncover something they were not meant to see. The shadows cast by the light created an eerie, almost theatrical effect, heightening the suspense that enveloped them.

Léonie steadied herself, her hand instinctively resting on the service pistol at her side. Nicolas, though unarmed, stood resolute, his curiosity mingling with a growing sense of foreboding.

They stood in silence for a moment, the light from the studio casting hard shadows in the alley. The quiet was oppressive, filled with the potential of hidden truths and lurking danger. The door, now illuminated, seemed to beckon them, promising answers yet warning of risks untold.

Taking a deep breath, Léonie stepped forward.

7

"Are you certain this is the place?" asked Nicolas, his voice barely audible above the distant peal of church bells. His eyes darted up and down the darkened street as if expecting someone to leap out from the shadows and challenge their presence.

"Quite certain," replied Léonie, her gaze fixed upon the worn door. "There's only one way to find out what he knows."

With that, she raised her hand and rapped sharply on the door, the sound echoing through the narrow confines of the street. They waited for what felt like an eternity before the door creaked open, revealing the dimly lit interior of Gaston's studio.

"Ah, bonsoir, dear patron!" exclaimed Gaston, stepping into the light. His eyes twinkled with mischief as he took in their stern expressions, his lips curling into a knowing smile. "To what do I owe the pleasure of this unexpected visit?"

"Cut the pleasantries, Gaston," Léonie said curtly, her gaze fixed upon the motley assortment of canvases and sculptures that cluttered the room. "We have some questions about a painting, and it seems you may be the person to answer them."

"Ah, a painting!" Gaston's face lit up with genuine delight as though he had been waiting all his life for someone to ask him about art. "Very well, come inside and let us talk." He swept one arm grandly towards the interior of the studio, beckoning Nicolas and Léonie to follow him into the heart of the dimly lit space.

As they ventured further into the atelier, they could see that every surface was covered in art – from the great masters of the Renaissance to the modernists of the twentieth century. It was clear that Gaston Dupont was a man who not only loved art but lived and breathed it with every fibre of his being.

"Let's get straight to the point," said Nicolas, his voice firm and resolute. "We believe you may have information about the origins of a certain painting, a piece of artwork that may be linked to a brutal murder."

"Indeed?" Gaston arched one eyebrow, the corners of his mouth twitching with suppressed amusement. "And what, pray tell, is so extraordinary about this particular painting that it warrants such a late-night visit?"

"Enough games," Léonie interjected, her patience wearing thin. "The question is, will you help us uncover the truth behind it?"

Gaston paused momentarily, his eyes flitting between Nicolas and Léonie as if weighing their sincerity. And then, with a soft chuckle, he nodded his assent.

"Very well, my friends," he said, his voice low and conspiratorial. "Let me have a look at this enigmatic painting and see what secrets it may reveal."

Gaston's eyes wandered over the photo Nicolas held

up before him. He hesitated, an almost imperceptible frown creasing his brow.

Gaston Dupont's studio was a labyrinth of canvases and art supplies, an eclectic mix of the new and the old that reflected the complex character of its owner. As Nicolas presented the mundane painting they had come to inquire about, Gaston's eyes flickered with a hint of recognition, albeit not one of admiration.

"Ah, that piece," Gaston began, his tone dismissive, almost embarrassed. "It was a commission from a client. Honestly, it's not something I'm particularly proud of. My heart wasn't in it, you see. Just a piece to pay the bills."

Léonie, seizing the opportunity, leaned in. "And who was this client, Mr. Dupont? It's crucial for our investigation."

Gaston, however, was deft in his deflection. With a wave of his hand, he turned their attention away from the question and towards his current projects. "Let's not dwell on past mediocrities. Allow me to show you what I'm truly passionate about."

As he led them through the dimly lit studio, his swift steps expertly navigating the labyrinth of art, he showcased an array of masterpieces that left them speechless. Each piece's vibrant colours and intricate details were nothing short of breathtaking, a testament to the artist's skill and dedication. So precise were the recreations that they could easily be mistaken for the original works, each stroke perfectly mirrored in flawless harmony. It was as if they had stepped into a world where every brushstroke held its own story, waiting to be discovered by eager eyes and curious minds.

Nicolas, impressed yet sceptical, pointed out the uncanny resemblance. "These are remarkably like the old masters. One might even mistake them for…"

Gaston cut him off, a slight edge of pride in his voice. "Reproductions, not forgeries. I study the masters to honour their techniques, to understand their genius. It's a form of homage, really."

Léonie couldn't help but grunt in response. "As exquisite as these are, they walk a fine line. It's only when a reproduction is signed with a forged signature, pretending to be someone else's work, that it becomes a forgery."

Gaston nodded, acknowledging the point. "Exactly, Inspector. And I would never cross that line. My reproductions are sold as what they are, an artist's tribute to the greats. Never under false pretences."

"Gaston," Nicolas began, his voice firm yet laced with curiosity, "we've marvelled at your reproductions, but what of this piece you've hidden? What's its story?"

Gaston looked at the photo Nicolas showed him, the painting that was found underneath. A playful smile danced on Gaston's lips. "Ah, you have an eye, Nicolas. That one? It's a piece shrouded in mystery, much like the stories surrounding the old masters." His answer was a tapestry of intrigue and evasion, spun with the skill of a seasoned storyteller.

Nicolas pressed on, undeterred. "Where did it come

from? What do you know about it?" His questions pierced the air, aiming to unravel the riddles that Gaston wove.

Gaston took the photo from Nicolas, his hands hovering over it with a magician's flair. "It came to me as all great art does, through a series of curious events and mysterious benefactors," he said, his voice blending amusement and secrecy. "Its origins are as layered as the paint upon its surface."

Nicolas's frustration grew, but before he could probe further, Gaston turned his charm towards Léonie. "Inspector, surely you appreciate the allure of the unknown? Some pieces carry their value not in their provenance but in the stories they inspire."

Léonie, unswayed by Gaston's attempts to enchant, maintained her focus. "Stories are fascinating, Mr. Dupont, but in our line of work, facts hold the key to unlocking mysteries."

"Don't let the facts mislead you, Inspector," Gaston winked.

"Who gave you the painting?" Léonie pressed on.

Gaston sighed, theatrically resigning himself to their persistence. "It was a gift from an admirer of my work who wished to remain anonymous. They felt it would be 'right at home' among my collection."

His explanation, wrapped in vagueness, did little to satisfy their quest for answers.

Seeing Gaston's reluctance to divulge more, Nicolas shifted strategies. "Gaston, any piece of art in your possession surely has a tale worth telling. This painting has been stolen from my shop, and a man has lost his life for it. Can't you tell us anything?"

Gaston's eyes narrowed slightly, a flicker of caution passing through them. "Art connects us in mysterious ways, doesn't it? Perhaps what you seek is not the origin of the art but its essence." His response, while poetic, skirted the heart of Nicolas's inquiry.

Léonie, sensing the conversation was veering into circles, decided on a direct approach. "Mr. Dupont, cooperation with our investigation could shed light on your admirer and clear any shadows cast over this painting's presence..."

She was interrupted by a catchy melody coming from the phone in her pocket. Looking at the caller's name, she sighed and stepped aside.

"Police Chief Moreau?" she said, lifting an eyebrow, expecting nothing good of his call.

"Inspector Martens," the Police Chief began, his voice heavy with disappointment, "I have just received word that our request for a search warrant has been denied."

"Denied?" Léonie inquired, her green eyes flashing with frustration. "On what grounds?"

"Apparently," Moreau explained, "the judge deemed our evidence insufficient to establish probable cause for a search."

Nicolas clenched his fists involuntarily as he studied Léonie's frustration. They had come so close, only to be thwarted by bureaucracy. The setback was disheartening, but their determination remained undiminished.

"Very well, Chief Moreau" Léonie replied, her tone resolute."We shall find another way to uncover the truth behind this murder…"

"Martens, there may be an opening," he continued, pausing for dramatic effect. "We have received word of an upcoming event at the law firm. They are hosting a party this weekend, and with many high profile clients on the guest list the police will have a presence."

"Moreau, what are you suggesting?" Léonie asked, her interest piqued.

"An opportunity, Inspector," he responded, his gaze unwavering. "You could work undercover as police security for the event. It would grant you access to potential leads and perhaps even the answers we seek."

Léonie considered the proposal, her mind racing through scenarios and potential outcomes. She knew the dangers of going undercover, but the allure of new information was tempting. Her instincts told her that the party could hold the key to cracking the case wide open.

"Alright," she finally agreed, her resolve evident in her measured tone. "I'll do it."

"Agreed," Chief Moreau confirmed. "I'll arrange it."

Léonie put the phone back in her pocket and stepped up to Gaston Dupont, staring him in the eyes.

"Well, Monsieur Dupont," she said, her tone hard and unwavering. "Either you tell us what you know here and now, or I'll escort you to an interrogation room at the station. What will it be?"

Gaston did not reply; his gaze flickered around the

studio. His cocky attitude and chivalrous manners faded from his demeanour. Then he swallowed hard, took a step back and met her gaze.

"Tell me, Inspector Martens," he purred. "What is it about this painting that has captured your imagination? Is it the history? The craftsmanship? Or perhaps it's the thrill of the chase itself?"

"Your charm may be disarming, Mr. Dupont," Léonie retorted, refusing to be swayed by his flirtations, "but it does not change the fact that we are here to uncover the truth behind this painting."

"Ah, la vérité," Gaston mused, tracing a finger along the edge of a nearby easel. "Now there's a concept with many layers, much like the varnish on a priceless masterpiece."

"Enough with the riddles," Léonie snapped. "We need answers, not more questions. Come here!" She grabbed his arm. "You'll have to accompany me to the police station."

"Very well," Gaston acquiesced, a wry smile playing upon his lips. "I will tell you what you need, but my clientele value discretion…"

"Go on now!" Léonie demanded.

"It's not often I find myself in the company of such dedicated protectors of art and history…and the truth," Gaston began, his gaze lingering on Léonie with an appreciation that bordered on the theatrical. "Perhaps a small token of my esteem for your efforts is in order."

Léonie, accustomed to the dance of interrogation, met

his gaze evenly. "Your cooperation would be the most valued token, Mr. Dupont."

Gaston chuckled, the sound rich and warm. "Very well, Inspector. Let's peel back a layer of this mystery, shall we?" He paused as if weighing the consequences of his following words. "The client, or rather the messenger of my mysterious benefactor, was a young man. Very slim, cloaked in the anonymity of a black hoodie. He was... how shall I put it? Ephemeral, almost ghostlike in his presence."

Nicolas leaned in, his interest piqued. "This man, did he say anything about the painting? Anything that might hint at its importance?"

"If only he had," Gaston sighed. "Our exchange was devoid of pleasantries or explanations. He simply requested that the old painting be covered by a new one I was to create. A curious commission, but not entirely unheard of in the circles that appreciate the... transformative power of art."

"And when he returned?" Léonie pressed, sensing the narrative's undercurrents.

"When he returned," Gaston continued, "it was as if the shadows themselves had parted to bring him back to my doorstep. He collected the completed piece with the same air of mystery that accompanied its arrival. No name, no trace, just the fleeting connection between artist and patron."

Throughout the exchange, Gaston's attempts to charm Léonie were persistent. Yet, she navigated his advances with a professionalism that spoke of her dedication to the case.

"Mr. Dupont, while the enigmatic nature of your client is certainly intriguing, it's the painting that holds the key. Anything else you can recall could prove invaluable."

Gaston, caught in the crossfire of duty and desire, finally capitulated. "Inspector, I fear I've told you all I know. This young man, this messenger, was a phantom in the grand tapestry of art patrons. Yet, it's clear the piece he brought me was more than mere canvas and paint—it was a vessel for something greater, perhaps even dangerous."

As they prepared to leave, Gaston offered Léonie a parting glance, one that promised stories untold and secrets yet to be uncovered. "Art, Inspector, like beauty, often lies in the eye of the beholder. What you seek may not always be visible on the surface."

As they left the dimly lit studio, a sense of anticipation hung in the air, charged with the promise of unravelling secrets and unmasking deceptions. The stage was set for a night that would test their resolve and challenge their understanding of the world they thought they knew. Nicolas' heart was racing with equal parts trepidation and excitement. A new chapter was about to unfold, and with it, the hope of unearthing long-buried secrets and bringing justice to those who had been wronged.

8

The bell above the door of Nicolas De Wever's antique shop tinkled, a delicate herald announcing he had returned to his realm of history and artistry. The past day's events and disasters lingered in the back of his mind, but he forced it down, and with a solemn nod, he welcomed the trickle of customers that soon swelled into a steady stream. Each revealed themself more as a visitor shadowed by their curiosity than a potential customer. The air of the small shop was thick with whispers and sidelong glances, customers eagerly searching for any clues or signs of the recent crime that had shaken the peaceful neighbourhood. The air was heavy with a sense of mystery and intrigue as everyone tried to piece together the events of that fateful night.

"Murder most foul," an elderly woman murmured, her voice carrying the weight of the morning's headlines. She fingered the edge of a Louis XV console table, glancing up at Nicolas through a veil of suspicion and intrigue. "And in such a respectable establishment as yours."

Nicolas, tall and slender like one of his nineteenth-century grandfather clocks, offered a measured smile. His blue eyes, sharp and discerning, held her gaze just long enough to acknowledge her statement without indulging it.

"Tragedy always seems to strike where least expected,

Madame," he replied, the timbre of his voice smooth as the varnish on his antiques.

Another patron, a portly gentleman with a taste for Flemish tapestries, leaned closer, his eyes gleaming with unspoken questions. "They say nothing was taken but the smallest of trinkets," he said conspiratorially. "Yet Dirk Meijer, gone..."

"Indeed, it is perplexing," Nicolas conceded, his words carefully chosen as he adjusted a display of ornate snuff boxes. He gave nothing away, yet his demeanour suggested a depth of knowledge just beneath the surface. Each response was calculated to maintain a delicate balance between transparency and the preservation of mystery.

The shop had become a theatre, and Nicolas, its reluctant star, cast in a play of hushed tones and curious glances. He moved gracefully among his patrons, the custodian of treasures and secrets alike. His suits, always impeccably tailored, spoke of a refinement that was echoed in the curated collection surrounding him.

"Surely you must have some clue, Monsieur De Wever," pressed a young woman with an eager light in her eyes. She stood beside a Renaissance bronze sculpture, her youth a stark contrast to their ancient patina.

"Clues, Mademoiselle, are often hidden in plain sight," Nicolas replied, directing her attention to a painting of a pastoral scene, its bucolic tranquillity belying the turmoil that occupied their thoughts. "But it takes a keen eye to discern them."

As the clock struck noon, Isabella breezed into the shop, her backpack slung over one shoulder and a determined look in her eyes. After a long morning of classes, she retreated to the backroom, eager to continue working on their latest acquisitions. She was soon lost in work, the buzz from the morning's lectures fading. Time seemed to stand still as she poured all her passion and creativity into each item, determined to make them perfect. And as the sunlight filtered through the small window, illuminating her workspace, Isabella couldn't help but feel content and fulfilled in this little corner of the world where she could let her imagination run wild.

The morning waned, giving way to the afternoon, and with it, the crowd began to thin. Hushed conversations became less frequent, and Nicolas could feel the collective anticipation ebbing away, leaving behind only the silent watchfulness of the objects in his care.

As the last customer stepped out, the chime of the bell rang once more, marking an end to the performance. Nicolas let out a breath he hadn't realised he was holding. Now devoid of life other than his own, the shop seemed to exhale with him.

He straightened a displaced book spine, his movements deliberate, his resolve unyielding. The case was far from closed, and in the silence of his shop, surrounded by echoes of the past, he was ready to delve deeper into the mystery that had unwittingly chosen him as its historian.

"Nicolas, what's this?" Isabella asked, holding up the

note with a curious tilt of her head. Her appearance from the backroom brought a halt to his brooding.

Nicolas, caught slightly off guard, took a deep breath before responding.

"I found that hidden inside the old frame we were discussing the other day," he explained his tone a mix of reluctance and necessity. "It was concealed in a secret compartment."

Isabella's brows furrowed, a shadow of disappointment crossing her features. "You didn't mention this when I asked about the compartment," she pointed out, her voice carrying a tinge of hurt. It was rare for Nicolas to withhold things from her, and this omission stung.

Nicolas sighed, the weight of the investigation momentarily pressing down on him. "I know, and I'm sorry. It was a decision made at the moment, influenced by the police. They thought it best to keep certain details under wraps for the time being."

Isabella, though not fully appeased, nodded in understanding. The complexity of the situation, with its intertwining of art, history, and crime, was becoming increasingly apparent. "I guess that makes sense," she conceded, though her smile didn't quite reach her eyes.

Then, as she examined the note again, her demeanour shifted from disappointment to intrigue. "You know, this looks like an old book cipher," she mused, her academic interest piqued. "My friend and I used to create messages like this as children. It relies on two copies of the same book. The numbers correspond to pages, lines, and words to decipher the message."

Nicolas leaned in, his curiosity overtaking the earlier awkwardness. "Really? That sounds incredibly intricate. Do you think you could explain more about how it works?"

Isabella brightened, eager to share her knowledge. "Certainly. For example, the sequence 23-5-2 could mean page 23, line 5, word 2 in the book. Both the sender and receiver need the same edition of the book for it to work. It's a clever way to send hidden messages, almost impossible to crack without knowing the exact book used as the key."

Nicolas marvelled at the simplicity yet effectiveness of such a cipher. "That's fascinating, Isabella. It gives us a new angle to consider. Perhaps this note isn't as impenetrable as we thought. The challenge now is finding the book it's linked to."

Isabella's enthusiasm was contagious, and for a moment, the shop felt like a haven of discovery rather than a scene connected to crime. "Let's not lose hope," she said, a spark of determination in her eyes. "Maybe together, we can unravel this mystery."

The chime above the door announced another visitor. With a flourish of her scarf, Claire Dubois sashayed into the antique shop. Her smile danced with mischief as she perused the collection of relics that spoke of bygone eras, her gaze finally resting on Nicolas.

"Mon cher Nicolas," she cooed, "I hear your recent

misfortune has become a convenient clearance sale."Her laughter tinkled like fine crystal, light-hearted yet edged with the sharpness of an inside joke known only to those who frequented the clandestine circles of Brussels' high society.

Nicolas offered a polite smile that didn't quite reach his discerning blue eyes."Claire, always a pleasure to see you indulge in such whimsy,"he replied, maintaining his composure. He was accustomed to the playful banter that often accompanied the more affluent clients—those who viewed art as much as a social game as a cultural pursuit.

"Ah, but I jest," Claire said, her voice softening as she traced a finger along the frame of a seventeenth-century painting, her touch as delicate as if caressing a lover."The tragic loss of Dirk Meijer... now that I cannot make light of."

With the mention of the esteemed art historian, the air in the room seemed to grow heavier—a silent tribute to the man whose life had revolved around unravelling the mysteries of masterpieces. Nicolas noted the subtle change in her demeanour, a cloud passing over her usually radiant visage.

"Dirk was a pillar amongst us, his knowledge unparalleled," Claire continued her eyes momentarily losing their usual spark. "His passion for the art world was infectious, even to those of us who merely dabble on the fringes."

Nicolas nodded in agreement, feeling an unexpected kinship with Claire at that moment. Dirk Meijer's death was not just a loss to the academic community but to anyone who had ever been touched by the profound beauty of art's history.

"His legacy will no doubt endure through the works he loved so deeply. And now it is a matter for the police," Nicolas said, his voice as much a homage to the fallen historian as to the timeless pieces that adorned his shop.

"Indeed," Claire murmured, withdrawing her hand from the artwork. She turned back to Nicolas, the veil of sadness lifting as the habitual playfulness returned to her eyes. "And what did that police want with you earlier that day, tracing stolen art?" A mischievous smile played over her thin red lips.

As Nicolas did not bite, she shrugged. "Not any of my business; I shall leave you to your treasure trove, Nicolas. Do keep me informed if any more... intriguing incidents occur."

"Of course," he assured her, watching as she glided towards the door, her presence a reminder of the enigmatic dance between art and its beholders.

As the door closed behind her, leaving only the echo of the bell and the scent of her perfume, Nicolas felt the weight of the cipher hidden within Isabella's desk. The threads of the past were tangling with the present, and somewhere in the intricate weave lay the answers they sought. He turned the sign on the door to 'Closed' with a steady hand, securing a moment's peace amid chaos. The grandfather clock in the corner of the room struck six times, its resonant chimes echoing through the antique shop like a call to repose.

Isabella Leclerc slipped through the door behind him, her presence a gentle reminder of the world outside the intricacies of Flemish tapestries and Renaissance bronzes – and mysterious ciphers and crime.

"Any idea what the key might be?" Nicolas asked, his tone casual yet laden with expectancy.

The air between them felt charged with the thrill of the chase, the pursuit of truth hidden within the intricate dance of art and history.

"Nothing comes to mind just yet," Isabella confessed, but the spark in her eyes belied the gears turning in her head. It was only a matter of time before a fragment of memory would guide them to the doorway of revelation. After all, every code had its counterpart, every lock its key – and Isabella had stated that it was virtually impossible to decode a book cipher without the book.

"We'll look at it with fresh eyes in the morning," Nicolas encouraged her, his confidence in her abilities unwavering. "Thank you, Isabella. See you tomorrow."

She nodded and left the shop without further words.

*

Nicolas De Wever sought refuge in the familiar comforts of his flat above the shop. The evening was his to reclaim, a precious respite from the whirlwind of puzzles and enigmas that had entangled him. He decided to cook a two-course meal, an endeavour that always served to ground him and take his mind off the complexities of his world.

For the starter, Nicolas opted for a classic Belgian endive salad; its slightly bitter leaves a perfect counterbalance to the sweet and tangy dressing he whipped up from scratch. He topped it with crumbled walnuts and slices of crisp apple, the combination of flavours and textures promising a refreshing beginning to his solitary feast.

The main course was a heartier affair: a succulent coq au vin. Nicolas took his time browning the chicken to perfection before slowly simmering it in a rich sauce of red wine, with a bouquet garni, pearl onions, and button mushrooms lending depth and warmth to the dish. The wine, a robust Burgundy, infused the chicken with a complexity that only a slow cooking process could evoke.

With the meal prepared, Nicolas poured himself a glass of the same Burgundy used in the coq au vin. Its deep, velvety notes perfectly complemented the meal and a well-deserved indulgence. As he sat down to eat, the flavours of each dish mingled harmoniously, a testament to the care and passion he put into their creation.

The meal served its purpose, allowing Nicolas a momentary escape from the pressures of the investigation. But as he finished his last bite and savoured the final sip of wine, the reality of his situation settled back upon him—the fate of his laptop, the shadowy law firm, and the elusive art forger, Gaston Dupont.

With a sigh, he leaned back in his chair, allowing his blue eyes to drift closed momentarily. The scenes replayed in his mind, each more puzzling than the last: Dirk Meijer lying still amidst a fortress of knowledge, the stolen artwork spirited away into the night, the locked door that guarded more than just antiques.

In this moment of quiet reflection, Nicolas's thoughts wandered to the cryptic note found in the frame, its sequence of numbers a riddle yet unsolved. He pondered over Isabella's explanation of the book cipher, a method of encryption both ingenious and quaint, reliant on the shared knowledge of a specific text. The simplicity and historical nature of the cipher appealed to Nicolas's love for the past, a reminder of the days when secrets were hidden in plain sight within the pages of a book.

As he mulled over this connection, his mind inadvertently drifted to the various items and artworks that had passed through his shop over the years. Then, like a bolt out of the blue, it appeared before him – a frozen moment that Isabella had captured a few days ago. A uniformed man handing a book to another whose wooden leg marked him as Jean-Joseph Charlier.

Fumbling with the fabric of his jacket pocket, Nicolas retrieved his mobile. He zoomed in on the transferred tome, his breath catching as though he had ascended the grand staircase of history too quickly. The title, decorated in gold leaf against the leather cover, read "Le Dernier Jour d'un Condamné", and a thrill shot through him, electrifying his senses with the promise of understanding.

"Victor Hugo..." he murmured under his breath, the

revelation igniting a spark of urgency."The Last Day of a Condemned Man."

His fingers tapped frantically on the glossy screen of his smartphone, summoning the familiar number with a jittery urgency. The room pulsated with energy as he paced back and forth like a frantic conductor before an impatient orchestra, each step echoing like a drumbeat of desperation.

9

Two hours earlier, Léonie Martens stood before her full-length mirror, meticulously adjusting the lapels of her tailored black blazer. The fabric was soft and supple—chosen for both its elegance and ease of movement, a necessary blend for the night's assignment. She paired it with sleek trousers and a crisp white blouse, an ensemble that whispered sophistication without shouting authority. Her short curls were tamed into a polished look, a stray tendril rebelliously framing her determined green eyes.

"Remember," she murmured to her reflection, practising the firm yet measured tone of a security professional, "I'm here to oversee the safety of tonight's esteemed gathering." She refined each detail until it felt as comfortable as her own skin.

The grand entrance of Verhaegen & Delacroix Advocaten buzzed with subdued excitement as guests began to arrive in a parade of luxury vehicles and designer attire. The law offices had been transformed for the occasion. Each corner boasted a different treasure—a bronze statue from the Renaissance period here, a delicate Flemish tapestry there—all lending an air of cultural gravitas to the festivities.

As Léonie made her way through the crowd, she noted how the guests navigated the space, their movements choreographed by an unspoken understanding of status and influence. Corporate leaders engaged in hushed conversations, heads nodding with gravitas at each shared insight. Artists, identifiable by their flamboyant gestures and bohemian flair, animatedly discussed their latest creations. Actors, the very picture of grace, exchanged pleasantries with a practised charm that blurred the line between performance and genuine interest. And politicians, ever the tacticians, wove through the assembly, their calculated smiles stretching just wide enough to seem sincere.

Léonie's gaze lingered on the antique vases that flanked the entrance—Ming dynasty if she wasn't mistaken. Nicolas De Wever had provided many of the antiquities, his knowledgeable eye no doubt discerning the subtlest nuances of each piece. But her thoughts of him were fleeting; the hum of conversation served as a reminder of the task at hand.

The atmosphere was one of cultivated refinement, guests sipping champagne from slender flutes as they admired the artworks adorning the office. It was a scene that required poise and discretion, qualities Léonie possessed in spades. However, beneath the veneer of high culture, her senses remained alert. For amidst the laughter and the clinking of glasses lay the potential for clues—or danger—in the most sophisticated of settings.

Léonie glided through the congregation of Brussels' elite with the grace of a swan, her posture erect yet unassuming. The soft rustle of her chiffon gown blended with the symphony of hushed tones and delicate laughter that filled the air of the opulent law offices. She feigned admiration for an exquisite oil painting that hung above the marble mantelpiece, a convenient vantage point to survey the room while engaging in light banter with a gentleman whose eyes shone with the fervour of his passion.

"Remarkable, isn't it?" Léonie murmured, tilting her head slightly as she followed the collector's gaze to the artwork. "Do you happen to know who advised on these pieces? The curation is impeccable."

"I'm afraid such details escape me. I focus on the art, not on those who choose to display it," he replied with a polite but distant smile.

She continued, approaching a group of well-dressed individuals.

"Excuse me," Léonie began her tone both courteous and firm, "I'm looking for information on the decorator responsible for these remarkable renovations. Would any of you happen to know their name?"

Her seemingly innocuous question was met with a sudden coolness, the air charged with an unspoken tension. Glances were exchanged, a silent communication that spoke volumes of the etiquette and discretion that governed these circles.

Undeterred, Léonie approached other guests, her query repeated with unwavering resolve. Yet, the responses were frustratingly similar, a chorus of polite deflections and veiled dismissals. "The decorator? A trivial matter, surely. Have you seen the latest acquisition by the museum?"

As she excused herself from the conversation with a polite smile, her attention was drawn to a man who commanded the space around him with an effortless magnetism. Pascal Charlier, flanked by admirers, laughed heartily, the timbre of his voice rich and inviting. His dark hair, peppered with distinguished streaks of silver, lay neatly combed back, accentuating the confident set of his jaw. He was dressed impeccably in a tailored suit that whispered luxury without shouting wealth—a fine line treaded only by those accustomed to the spotlight.

By his side stood a catwalk beauty, her arm looped through his in an elegant display of companionship. Her presence seemed almost ornamental against Pascal's stature. Yet, there was a sharp intelligence in her eyes that suggested she was far more than mere decoration. Completing the trio was a short, slim man whose quiet demeanour starkly contrasted with the animated and vibrant persona of Pascal Charlier. Clad in an impeccably tailored suit that whispered of sophistication and an understated confidence. In this crowd of lawyers and their clients, the man did not stand out for his attire, but for the air of introspection, he carried about him. With its subtle Italian stitching and sleek silhouette, the suit suggested meticulous attention to detail. At the same time, his contemplative expression lent him an enigmatic allure, making him a figure of intrigue among the opulence of the event.

As Pascal's laughter filled the air, a sound that seemed to effortlessly bridge gaps and draw people in, the slim man appeared almost removed from the moment, his attention seemingly captured by something beyond the immediate social exchanges. Under the thoughtful furrow of his brow, his eyes moved from one piece of artwork to another around the room, studying each with a keenness that suggested a deep appreciation or perhaps a search for something hidden within their frames. He seemed to exist in a world apart, where the conversations and laughter that ebbed and flowed around him were distant echoes.

A subtle but insistent nudge from Pascal broke the spell that the room seemed to have cast over the petit man. It was a silent reminder of the present, a call back to the reality of the gathering. Having momentarily captured Léonie's attention, Pascal's eyes sparkled with a mix of recognition and perhaps curiosity as she offered a nod in acknowledgment. Her surveillance was discreet but intent, cloaked beneath a veneer of casual interest that belied the sharpness of her observations.

The slim man, brought back from his reverie by Pascal's gesture, offered a small, almost imperceptible smile in response, a silent acknowledgement of his brief departure from the present. His adjustment was subtle, a slight straightening of posture and a more conscious engagement with his surroundings as if reorienting himself to the social landscape of the gathering. Yet, even as he rejoined the conversation, his earlier distraction and the depth of his engagement with the art around them lingered.

"Champagne, mademoiselle?" A waiter presented a tray to Léonie, and she accepted a glass without ever considering a zip. But a glass in her hand looked natural and unsuspicious as she drifted from one opulent cluster of guests to another, her ears as alert as her eyes. She lingered on the fringes of conversations that bubbled over with mentions of rare finds and restoration techniques, the subtle perfume of intrigue as intoxicating as the vintage champagne being sipped by the silver-haired guests.

Amidst the sibilant whispers and the delicate chime of crystal, the silent thrum of her mobile phone against her ribcage was like an erratic heartbeat. Once, twice, it buzzed, each vibration an insistent punctuation mark in the evening's script. Léonie acknowledged the intrusion with only the faintest dart of her eyes downward, betraying no sign of distraction. Her role as a security officer was a meticulously crafted facade, allowing her to navigate this sea of refinement with purpose.

Though laced with the scent of orchids and the warmth of soft lighting, the air grew heavy with something unspoken, a web of glances and gestures she was trained to decipher. As time pressed its weight upon her, the urgency to consult the device hidden within the folds of her elegant attire gnawed at her resolve.

"Excusez-moi," she murmured, extracting herself from a conversation about the provenance of a particular

Flemish tapestry. The words were dipped in regret but edged with necessity; her exit was as smooth as the silk of her gown.

With each step, Léonie wove through the crowd, her senses sharpened to the brink. The murmur of art enthusiasts discussing the merits of Baroque versus Renaissance, the soft laughter shared under the glow of antique chandeliers—each sound tethered her to her duty even as the buzzing of her phone beckoned.

She seized the moment as the crowd's attention latched onto a flamboyant toast by a visiting Italian opera director. She slipped through an archway draped in velvet and into the tranquillity of a book-lined study, the rich aroma of leather-bound volumes replacing the heady perfume of socialites. Her phone was a cold weight in her palm, its screen a mosaic of missed calls and urgent texts from Nicolas.

"Dammit," she murmured, thumbing the callback button with a sense of mounting urgency. The din of the party muffled the tones in her ear; the laughter and clinking glasses outside were a cacophony that throttled the connection. She angled her body, seeking refuge behind a towering mahogany bookcase as if it could shield her from the revelry and bolster the signal.

"Nicolas, it's Léonie," she spoke into the void, half-pleading for the call to breach through. "I'm here. Talk to me." But the line crackled and spat out silence, mocking her attempts.

Through the window, the Brussels skyline stood

indifferent, a silhouette of history against the twilight. Léonie pressed the phone to her ear once more before the call dissolved into nothingness. A leaden feeling settled in her stomach – time was slipping away, and somewhere in the city, the pieces of their puzzle were stirring without them.

*

Nicolas paced the length of his antiquities shop, the musty scent of old paper and varnished wood doing little to ease his frustration. His phone lay accusingly silent upon the counter. He had pieced together a thread, one so delicate yet vital, and Léonie was the linchpin to unravelling it further. Each tick of the antique grandfather clock was a taunt, a reminder of the chasm between discovery and dead end.

"Come on, Léonie," he muttered, willing his phone to life with each pass. His mind raced with the breakthrough; the cipher that had been a stubborn lock now swung open in his mind's eye. But the key, the meaning, it needed her sharp intuition, her tenacity to turn it entirely.

A car honked outside, a fleeting distraction from the oppressive wait. Nicolas ran a hand through his hair, strands of grey catching the soft light, betraying the hour. His shop, usually a sanctuary of art and history, felt like a gilded cage, trapping him with the knowledge he couldn't act upon alone.

He glanced toward Isabella's work desk, cluttered with research and scribbled notes, a testament to their shared quest. If only Léonie would answer, they could leap forward together. But for now, he was left pacing, a solitary figure in a room filled with silent witnesses of bygone eras.

Nicolas's hand hovered above the assortment of art reference books lining the shelves, his fingers brushing their leather-bound spines in a silent apology for neglecting them. Instead, he reached for the phone; its sleek modernity was an inconsistent presence in the antiquated ambience of his shop.

"Isabella," he spoke briskly as the call connected, "I have it. The cipher - I think I've cracked it."

On the other end, Isabella's voice danced with excitement. "Truly? That's incredible, Nicolas! What does it say?"

"Patience. We need Victor Hugo's 'Le Dernier Jour d'un Condamné'. I believe there's a copy at Claire Dubois's," he said, already reaching for his coat, the fabric whispering against the quiet of the shop. "I think I have to wake her up."

"I'll be there in twenty minutes," Isabella replied, the eagerness in her voice echoing his pulse of anticipation.

Together, they stood outside the glass facade of Claire Dubois's shop, their breaths forming fleeting clouds in the cool Brussels air. The book, that precious tome bound in faded burgundy leather, lay just beyond their reach, showcased amidst other literary treasures under the golden glow of strategically placed spotlights. As if sensing their urgency, the display seemed to beckon them, the gilded lettering on the book's spine shimmering like a beacon through the pane.

Claire came up behind them and unlocked the door with a curious smile.

Nicolas and Isabella stood in the dimly lit confines of Madame Claire Dubois's exclusive art collections, urgency etched into their expressions. Outside, the night had wrapped Brussels in its silent embrace, an unusual time for such a request. Yet, here they were, seeking an artefact of literature rather than art.

"Dear Claire," Nicolas began, his voice betraying the gravity of their visit, "we find ourselves in desperate need of a particular book – a first edition of Victor Hugo's work. It's crucial to our investigation."

Claire Dubois raised an eyebrow, her interest piqued by the late-hour plea. "A first edition Hugo? At this hour?" she teased, her tone a blend of amusement and curiosity. "What sort of mystery drives you to my doorstep for such a specific request?"

Isabella, ever the enthusiast, couldn't hide her excitement. "It's part of a cipher, Madame. We believe it holds the key to solving a case that's... well, it's unlike any other."

The request, unconventional as it was, delighted Claire. Her business was a treasure trove of gems of all art forms, and the idea of one of her items unlocking a real-world mystery was too enticing to resist.

"Very well," she said, a smile playing on her lips as she led them through the labyrinth of shelves. "But you must promise to tell me everything once this is all over. My books enjoy being part of a good story."

Moments later, she handed them the sought-after volume. "Ah, voilà!" exclaimed Isabella, her fingers reverently touching the cover as Claire placed the book in her hands. "This is it, Nicolas. This is our key."

Claire watched them, a mixture of satisfaction and curiosity lighting up her eyes. "I expect a full account, you hear?" she bantered, half-serious. "A book of mine playing detective is a tale I must hear."

Nicolas nodded, a smile of gratitude breaking through his earlier tension. "Of course, Claire. Your generosity tonight may well be the turning point in our investigation."

As they left with the book securely in Isabella's care, Claire Dubois stood at her doorway and watched them cross the street; she felt a sense of pride as her knowledge of art and antiques once again proved to be a sanctuary of answers in the most unexpected of ways.

Back in the safety of the shop, the two huddled over the counter, the book sprawled open between them. Nicolas's eyes skimmed the text, looking for the words, the hidden messages that had eluded them until now. Isabella read out the numbers of the cipher one after the other.

And then, as Nicolas read aloud the words decoded from the cipher, the atmosphere curdled from anticipation to perplexion. The French phrases tumbled nonsensically, a jumble of misplaced verbs and nouns. It started with:

"que Il de se on s'est d'un homme laissé une misérable manières jaunes rencontré compte inégaux" – "that he of himself was of a man left a miserable yellow manners met unequal account".

"It's not possible," Nicolas murmured his brow furrowing, eyes darting back and forth across the page as if the very letters would rearrange themselves under his scrutiny.

"Could it be a mistake?" Isabella ventured, her voice a tentative whisper against the thudding of their shared disappointment.

"No. The cipher was flawless; the translation was exact." He shook his head, the streaks of grey in his hair catching the light, a visual echo of his inner turmoil. "We are missing something. Maybe I was mistaken."

"An anagram, perhaps?" Isabella's suggestion cut through the heavy silence, her naiveté in other matters contrasted sharply by her astuteness in this realm of enigma.

"Or a code within a code," Nicolas pondered, the gears of his intellect once again set into motion by Isabella's inadvertent clue. They exchanged a glance, a silent agreement to delve deeper into the mystery that wound tightly around Victor Hugo's words.

"Let's try again," Nicolas suggested, determination stealing his voice as he reached for a notepad and pen. In the sanctuary of his shop, surrounded by the silent sentinels of art and history, they began anew, piecing

together the puzzle that refused to yield its secrets so
readily.

10

The sun rose over the rooftops, casting shadows that danced on the cobblestone streets of Brussels. Nicolas sat in a small corner café, nursing a lukewarm cup of coffee as his eyes wandered over the worn pages of the book. The warm, golden light filtering through the stained glass windows cast an array of colours onto the pages, illuminating the neat script inside. As he scanned the text again, he could not shake off the disappointment; it seemed that the book held no key to deciphering the encrypted note.

Léonie entered the café, her cheeks flushed from the brisk morning air. She ordered a cappuccino and slid into the seat opposite Nicolas; she began to speak in hushed tones, careful not to draw unnecessary attention. As the murmur of other patrons filled the room, Nicolas leaned in closer to hear her soft voice.

"The party at Verhaegen & Delacroix Advocaten was a bust," she said, disappointment evident in her tone. "The flamboyant decorator that we were hoping to meet was nowhere to be seen, and no one seemed to have any information about her."

She recounted the lacklustre events of the law firm's party, where nothing of significance had occurred. The air was thick with the scent of morning toast, coffee and fresh croissants, but there was a feeling of disappointment that clouded the table. Even their coffees had a tang of bitterness.

Nicolas let out a sigh and rubbed his temples as if trying to will away the headache that had been plaguing him all morning.

"I can unfortunately not make this morning any brighter," he began wearily. He explained how he had initially thought he had cracked the encrypted note, believing he had identified the book it was referencing. But despite his efforts, it proved to be in vain as his solution did not work. His disappointment was evident in his defeated tone.

Nicolas frowned, his eyes darting back to the book before returning to meet hers. "I was hoping this book would give us the answers we need, but it's been a dead end so far."

"Maybe we're approaching this from the wrong angle," Léonie suggested, her brow furrowed in thought. "We can't be certain that the book is meant to help us decode the note, though it must hold some significance."

"Perhaps," Nicolas conceded reluctantly, his fingers tracing the embossed cover absentmindedly. He couldn't shake off the feeling that the book was important, even if it wasn't directly linked to the note. "Perhaps we should go back to Gaston Dupont's studio. Maybe we missed something that could shed light on the painting's history."

The gentle clatter of porcelain cups and saucers seemed to underscore the urgency of their conversation. Léonie's gaze was drawn to a group of pigeons pecking at crumbs on the cobblestones, momentarily losing herself in the simplicity of their existence.

"It's worth a try," she replied, nodding her agreement. "We could also look more closely at Gaston's notes and sketches. There might be something there that can help us decipher the encrypted note."

"Exactly," Nicolas confirmed, feeling a renewed sense of determination. "There's bound to be something we've overlooked. Every clue matters now more than ever."

"True," Léonie admitted, her eyes betraying a hint of concern. "But let's proceed with caution. We're delving into dangerous territory, and I fear what we might uncover." She paused, a steely resolve settling over her features. "But we owe it to those who've lost their lives to find the truth."

"Agreed," Nicolas said solemnly, picking up the book and tucking it under his arm. He stood, signalling for the bill. As the waiter approached, Nicolas couldn't help but notice how ordinary everything seemed, how blissfully unaware the café patrons were of the sinister undercurrents swirling around them. "Let's go as soon as possible."

As they left the café and made their way towards Gaston Dupont's studio, he couldn't shake the feeling that they were stepping ever closer to a precipice from which there would be no return. But he also knew that he and Léonie wouldn't rest until justice was served.

*

heavy silence hung over Gaston Dupont's studio as Léonie pushed the door open. The day was grey and overcast, making the ample space dark and ominous. Nicolas followed her in, and a chill crept up his spine. His eyes scan the disarray with a palpable sense of unease. An overturned easel and scattered paintbrushes were the first he saw in the dim light.

Léonie's words were barely a whisper as she observed the scene before them. Their footsteps echoed in the empty room, their presence the only sign of life in this desolate place. "Something is very wrong here," she hissed, her eyes darting around for any sign of danger.

Nicolas tensed, his instincts on high alert as he surveyed the chaotic scene. The broken palette and overturned furniture spoke volumes – there had been a violent struggle...

"What could have caused such destruction? Was someone searching for something?" His voice was low, filled with unease at the thought of what dark events may have taken place within these walls.

But it was Léonie who made the most chilling discovery. Her flashlight illuminated a dark smear on the floor, likely blood. She approached it cautiously, her hand trembling as she reached for her weapon.

"This isn't good, Nicolas. I can feel it in my bones. We're walking into something dangerous."

As they moved further into the studio, the extent of the chaos became increasingly apparent. Canvases were slashed, frames were broken, and supplies were strewn haphazardly about the room. It was as if a whirlwind had ripped through the space, leaving devastation in its wake.

The air hung heavy with the stench of oil paints and turpentine, tainted by a faint coppery tang. Nicolas's nostrils flared as he stepped through the devastation towards Gaston's office at the back. Léonie led the way, her flashlight sweeping through the shadows.

"Nicolas, look," she whispered, pointing at a dark streak smeared across the floorboards. The beam of light caught something glistening in the irregular stain – blood.

"Stay behind me," she continued, her voice low and urgent. She edged forward, her body tense with anticipation. Every nerve hummed with foreboding, each creak of the floor beneath their feet echoing like a gunshot in the oppressive silence. They approached the office door, left slightly ajar.

"Stay back," Léonie commanded. Nicolas nodded, a steely determination etched upon his face. With a deep breath, Léonie pushed open the door.

The scene that greeted them was one of utter devastation. Documents lay torn and shredded on the floor; overturned furniture and streaks of paint mixed with blood across the wooden boards. And amidst the chaos, sprawled in a pool of viscous crimson, lay Gaston Dupont – lifeless.

"Mon Dieu…" Léonie gasped, the colour draining from her cheeks. She pulled up her phone, her fingers steady despite the chaos around them. "I'm calling for reinforcements."

"Good idea," Nicolas murmured, barely able to tear his gaze from the sight of the man they talked to just a few days ago. He couldn't believe what he was seeing. How had their search for answers led them here to this gruesome end?

"We've found a body," Léonie told the operator, her voice wavering. "Gaston Dupont... His studio. Please send someone right away. And we need a thorough analysis of the crime scene."

*

The echoes of sirens soon pierced the air, a cacophony of foreboding that crept under Nicolas's skin as he watched the police swarm Gaston Dupont's studio. Their methodical precision was a stark contrast to the chaos that had unfolded moments before.

"Inspector Martens," called a young officer, catching the attention of Léonie. "We've found something."

"Show me," Léonie demanded.

Nicolas couldn't help but glance over as the officer handed her a small plastic bag containing a pin. Even from a distance, he could make out the symbol emblazoned on it: a lion's head in black, yellow and red – the emblem of Belgium First.

"Interesting," Léonie murmured, examining the pin with furrowed brows. She looked up at the officer. "Where did you find this?"

"Underneath some fallen books near the body, Madame," the officer replied.

"Belgium First," Léonie whispered as she returned beside Nicolas, her eyes wide with disbelief. "What could that mean?"

"An interesting question," Nicolas mused, his mind racing with possibilities. Could Gaston have been involved with the controversial party? Or was it a clue left behind by the murderer?

"Did you get the feeling that Gaston had any involvement with the party?" Léonie asked.

"Never," Nicolas replied, his voice firm. "But that doesn't mean he wasn't involved, I suppose."

"Or it could be a red herring planted by the murderer," she suggested, her eyes narrowing. "We'll look into this further."

As the police ended their investigation, Nicolas couldn't help but feel a growing sense of unease. The discovery of the pin had only added more questions to the ever-increasing list of unknowns. The late afternoon sun cast long shadows in the small, cluttered room as Léonie paced back and forth, her fingers drumming against her thigh. Nicolas sat on the edge of a worn chair, tracing the edge of the pin with his fingertip, his brow furrowed in thought.

"Could Gaston have been involved with Belgium First?" Léonie asked, pausing in her pacing to study Nicolas' expression.

"Unlikely," he replied, his voice low and measured.

"Gaston was more interested in art than politics. But we must consider all possibilities."

"Then what about the murderer? Could they be affiliated with the party?" she probed, watching Nicolas turn the pin over in his hand.

"Perhaps." Nicolas hesitated, his gaze fixed on the small object as if it held the answers they sought. "But why leave the pin at the scene? To throw us off their trail? Or is there a deeper connection?"

"Maybe it's a warning," Léonie mused, her eyes narrowing. "Since we've been investigating the painting and its possible link to the party, this might be their way of telling us to back off."

"Or the murderer is attempting to frame the party," Nicolas added, his fingers drumming against the arm of the chair.

She nodded and sank slowly into a chair across from him

"Léonie," he said softly. "What if we're next?"

"Trust me, Nicolas, I won't let anything happen to you," she vowed, her eyes meeting his with unwavering determination. "We'll find the truth, and we'll bring whoever is responsible to justice."

"Even if it leads us into the lion's den?" he asked, a shiver of dread running down his spine.

"Especially then," she replied, her voice firm and confident.

As they sat in the fading light, the weight of their task pressing down on them, Nicolas and Léonie discussed the twisted threads connecting the painting, Gaston's murder, and the mysterious pin.

Léonie's hands trembled ever so slightly as she dialled the number for the police chief, her voice steady and determined despite the racing thoughts that threatened to overwhelm her. Nicolas stood nearby, his eyes never leaving hers, offering silent support.

"Chief Moreau, it's Inspector Martens," she began, her tone firm. "I have a request – we need to speak with Pascal Charlier, the leader of Belgium First."

"Charlier?" The Chief's voice crackled through the phone, a mixture of surprise and apprehension. "What on earth do you want with him?"

"We believe there may be a connection between the party and Gaston Dupont's murder," Léonie explained, swallowing hard. "We've also uncovered evidence suggesting that the stolen painting might depict one of Charlier's ancestors, the revolution hero."

"Are you certain about this?" Chief Moreau asked, his voice heavy with concern.

"Nothing is certain, but we must explore every possibility," Léonie insisted, her heart pounding. "Please grant us permission to question him."

"Very well," the Chief sighed, relenting. "But be careful. Charlier is not someone to be trifled with."

"Thank you, Sir. We'll proceed cautiously," Léonie assured him, ending the call.

They left the studio behind. The shadows of the night seemed to slither and twist around them as they walked the deserted streets, the faint echo of their footsteps a reminder of the danger lurking behind every corner.

As they walked in silence, Léonie's mind raced with questions, her thoughts tumbling over one another in a whirlwind of confusion and fear. What was the true motive behind Gaston's murder? How did the painting fit into it all? And what would they uncover when they finally confronted Pascal Charlier?

"Nicolas," she said, her voice trembling slightly, "we need to regroup and rethink our strategy. We've stumbled upon something far more dangerous than we initially suspected. We must proceed with caution."

"We cannot afford any missteps," replied Nicolas, his voice steady and unwavering. "Perhaps we should go home, get some well-deserved sleep, gather our thoughts and explore different avenues of inquiry separately. We can reconvene tomorrow and share our findings."

"Very well," Léonie agreed, her mind racing with the implications of their discovery. She hated the idea of parting ways, especially when danger seemed ever-present, but she knew that Nicolas was right. They needed to cast a wider net if they were to uncover the truth behind Gaston's murder and the mysterious painting.

"Promise me one thing, Nicolas," Léonie implored, her eyes searching his face for reassurance. "Promise me you'll be careful. I have a terrible feeling about all of this, and I don't want anything to happen to you."

"Nor I to you, Léonie," Nicolas responded, his gaze unwavering. "I promise we will both tread lightly but persistently. Let us vow to uncover the truth behind this painting and bring justice to those responsible for the murders, no matter the cost."

"Agreed," Léonie whispered, unable to suppress the shiver that ran down her spine as she uttered the words.

With a final nod of resolve, they parted ways, each disappearing into the enveloping darkness, their hearts heavy with the knowledge that there was no turning back. As Léonie walked towards her apartment, the chilling sensation of being watched seemed to cling to her like a shadow, and she couldn't help but wonder if the hunter had indeed become the hunted.

11

The first light of dawn filtered through the lace curtains as Nicolas De Wever stirred from his slumber. A weightless sense of well-being filled him, a testament to the previous night's uninterrupted sleep. With great contentment, he stretched his long limbs beneath the crisp linen sheets, relishing in the rare luxury of a refreshing morning.

After dressing in a tailored suit, Nicolas prepared a modest breakfast of tea, toast, and soft-boiled eggs. The fragrant aroma of the freshly brewed Earl Grey wafted through the air, wrapping him in a warm embrace that only heightened his enthusiasm for the day ahead. As he enjoyed his meal, his mind wandered to the mysterious painting and its elusive secrets.

"Today," he mused, "I shall uncover the truth."

With renewed determination, Nicolas made his way down to his shop. He unlocked the door, flipped the sign to 'Open', and felt comfort in the familiar scent of aged wood and ancient artefacts.

While he waited for the first customer to step over the threshold, his mind settled on the enigmatic subject: Jean-Joseph Charlier, whose mysterious history seemed to follow him with an uncanny intensity.

"Good morning, Monsieur Wooden Leg," Nicolas

murmured as he zoomed into the photograph of the painting. "Let us see what more secrets you hold."

Under the gentle glow of the overhead lights, Nicolas meticulously examined the artwork on the photo again and then its frame, searching for any hidden details or clues that may have been overlooked. His sharp blue eyes scanned the surface, pausing at every subtle nuance of colour and technique. He peered closely at the delicate brushstrokes that captured the men's expressions. He could not find anything new, and he felt a growing sense of frustration. Each detail and each stroke seemed to mock his efforts to unravel the mystery that had consumed him.

As his gaze wandered over the image, the delicate signature at the bottom corner caught his attention again. It was a silent witness to the artist's identity. And then, just as silently, the year beside it whispered its significance: 1831. The year the revolution ended, a year fraught with historical weight and untold stories. But?

With a surge of urgency, Nicolas fetched Hugo's book, the potential key to deciphering the cryptic note they had found. He flipped it open to the first page, his hands trembling slightly with anticipation. And there it was. Published by Eugène Renduel, Paris, 1932.

1932. This book could never be the key to the book cipher. He had been mistaken all along. Nicolas's mind raced as he sought to understand the connection. Was there an elusive thread that could tie everything together?

He took a step back, his heart racing with excitement

as the implications of his discovery took root. The puzzle had changed, but there was also a new piece that had revealed itself – even understanding that a piece was wrong was a step forward, a small step forward. He could hardly wait to delve further into the mystery that seemed to envelop Charlier like a shroud.

"Isabella will want to hear of this," he thought, reaching for his phone. "We're one step closer to solving the riddle."

Nicolas couldn't help but feel an exhilarating sense of anticipation as he dialled her number. The truth behind the enigmatic painting was within reach, and he was determined to uncover it, no matter what secrets lay hidden within its depths.

*

The soft chime of the antique clock echoed through Nicolas's shop as he locked the door behind him, cradling the book borrowed from Claire Dubois. A gentle breeze rustled the leaves in the quaint street outside, creating a soothing soundtrack to his thoughts. It had been a fruitful morning with the revelation of the painting's origin year, and now it was time to return the book that had set them on this path.

"Ah, Nicolas! Back again so soon?" Claire greeted him warmly, her eyes twinkling with curiosity as she noticed the book under his arm. Her shop did not smell of antiques and old leather bindings, but of a posh perfume she used to attract her exclusive clientele – an aroma he found neither comforting nor invigorating.

"Is the police's investigation progressing?"

"Slowly but steadily," Nicolas lied, deliberately withholding last night's gruesome murder. "They've uncovered more, but there are still many questions left unanswered."

Claire studied him briefly, her eyes narrowing slightly as if assessing what he had told her. "Well," she said at last, nodding to the book he held against his chest, "did the book help you at all?"

"Unfortunately," he replied, placing the book on the counter. "It appears we were mistaken about this volume."

"Really?" She arched a delicate brow, her interest piqued. "Do tell."

Nicolas hesitated for a moment, weighing the pros and cons of revealing their setback. Ultimately, he chose honesty. "It seems that this book, while fascinating, isn't the key we were seeking. The painting we're researching was done in 1831, and this book was published after that."

"Did you know," she continued slowly, creating an air of suspense, "that there was an anonymous edition published in 1829, predating the one you've been studying? It wasn't until 1832 that Victor Hugo added his preface and put his name to the work."

"An anonymous edition?" Nicolas repeated, astonishment evident in his furrowed brow.

Nicolas felt his heart race with anticipation as the

weight of her words settled upon him. The prospect of unearthing a hidden truth, concealed for centuries within the pages of a forgotten book, invigorated him. He knew what he needed to do—find the original edition and unlock its secrets.

"Thank you, Claire," he murmured, his gaze unwavering. "I must find this early edition at once."

"Of course," she acquiesced, her lips curving into a knowing smile.

As he took his leave, Claire's words resonated within him, fortifying his resolve. The mystery that had trapped him now felt tantalisingly close to being unravelled, and he would not rest until he had discovered every last thread. With renewed determination, Nicolas De Wever set out to continue his quest, confident that the answers he sought lay hidden in the annals of history.

As he returned to the shop, Isabella was waiting for him, meeting him with an expectant gaze.

Nicolas filled her in with the last hour's revelations, that the book they used was newer than the painting and that there was a previous edition of the book, dating back to 1829.

"So, we've been misled all along?" Isabella wondered aloud, her concern evident in the furrow of her brow.

"Indeed, we have," Nicolas replied, his sharp blue eyes scrutinising the young woman before him. "The anonymous edition Claire mentioned, published in 1829... we must find it."

"Then let us begin our search anew," Isabella declared, determination shining in her eyes.

Nicolas studied her for a moment, appreciating the fierce loyalty and passion she brought to their pursuit of the truth. "Yes," he agreed solemnly, "we owe it to Dirk and all those whose lives have been touched by this tragedy. Let's start by contacting the rare book dealers we know."

In the empty shop, two steadfast hearts beat as one in their quest for answers. And though the path before them was shrouded in ambiguity, they embarked upon it with unwavering certainty, guided by their shared passion for art and history and the pursuit of justice.

The sun cast its golden rays on the meticulously arranged antiquities as Nicolas stood near his shop window, his mobile phone pressed to his ear.

"It's... it's rather urgent. You don't, huh? Could you possibly double-check? Maybe something's been misplaced, or... No, I get it, it's a long shot. ... Ah, you see, it's not just any book for me; it's the missing piece, the... No, I've been everywhere, every nook in this city. You were my... Yes, I understand your stock is extensive, but... No, no, of course, I didn't mean to imply... It's just that I'm running out of options here, and... Yes, I'll hold."

Nicolas sighed deeply, running a hand through his hair in frustration.

"Still nothing? Okay, okay. But if it turns up by some stroke of luck, you'll let me know. It's critical, tied to...

Well, it's a long story. Yes, that's my number. I appreciate this, truly. Thank you, anyway. Goodbye."

As they pursued the quest for the first edition of the book, their calls to local and international antiquarians were accompanied by the scratch of Isabella's pen on paper, each name scratched out as another futile call.

"Nicolas," Isabella hesitated, her pen poised above the paper. "Do you think the KBR have a copy of the original edition?"

"The Royal Library of Belgium is an excellent suggestion," he mused, a glimmer of hope in his blue eyes. "We should visit immediately. This could be the breakthrough we need."

*

Stepping into the modernised entrance of the Royal Library, Nicolas and Isabella were immediately enveloped by an atmosphere of innovation and elegance. The sleek glass facade reflected the cutting-edge design, a stark contrast to the ancient wisdom resting inside. As they passed through the automatic sliding doors, the subtle hum of technology in harmony with the quiet sanctity of knowledge greeted them. With every step into the brightly lit foyer, adorned with interactive displays and minimalist decor, they felt propelled into a new era of exploration. Here, amidst the fusion of tradition and technology, they sensed the thrilling possibility of uncovering unknown secrets, standing at the threshold of a new age of discovery.

"Excuse me," Nicolas addressed the librarian behind the information desk, his tone both polite and authoritative. "We are looking for a specific edition of a book – the original publication of Le Dernier Jour d'un Condamné from 1829. Might you have such a work in your collection?"

"Ah, yes," the librarian said, adjusting her glasses as she consulted the library's records. "We do have a copy of that particular edition. It is located in our rare books section. Follow me."

With their hearts pounding in unison, Nicolas and Isabella trailed the librarian through the halls and corridors, their eyes drinking in the boundless wealth of knowledge surrounding them. The air was thick with anticipation, and each step brought them closer to the answers they sought.

As the librarian unlocked the glass doors guarding the rare books section, Nicolas and Isabella exchanged glances, the weight of their shared purpose uniting them in this momentous pursuit. They had come this far, and now, armed with hope and determination, they stood prepared to face whatever secrets the elusive original edition might reveal.

The librarian delicately removed the original edition of Le Dernier Jour d'un Condamné from the shelf, her hands cradling the fragile spine with practised ease. The air within the rare books section seemed to crackle with anticipation; the silence was punctuated only by the whispering echo of turning pages.

"Here you are," she murmured, presenting it to Nicolas with reverence befitting its age and importance.

"Thank you," Nicolas said softly, his fingers tracing the worn leather binding as he took possession of the elusive book. Isabella peered over his shoulder, her eyes wide with wonder and curiosity.

"May we examine it here?" he asked, his voice barely audible in the hushed stillness of the room.

"Of course," the librarian acquiesced, gesturing towards a nearby table equipped with soft foam supports designed to protect the precious volumes during study.

As they settled into their seats, Nicolas and Isabella exchanged an electric glance, their hearts quickening with the thrill of discovery. Nicolas opened the book with bated breath, his keen blue eyes scanning the timeworn pages as Isabella carefully laid the note beside the book.

Isabella's eyes scanned the numbers as Nicolas carefully flipped through the pages, his heart racing. Beads of sweat formed on his forehead as he muttered to himself, connecting the dots. Isabella furiously scribbled down each piece of information, her hand cramping from the intensity. Suddenly, Nicolas slammed his hand down on the table and looked at her with a mixture of shock and realisation.

"It all makes sense now," he said breathlessly as she stopped reading. "This is the reason for Dirk Meijers' brutal murder.

*

In the muted ambience of Inspector Léonie Martens's office, the soft buzz of the overhead lights blended with the distant sounds of the police station, creating a backdrop that was both ordinary and charged with anticipation. The room, usually a place of order and clarity, seemed to take on a different character in the presence of her guests.

Léonie, seated not at the interrogation table but behind her desk cluttered with case files and notes, exuded a calm authority. Her sharp and discerning gaze rested on Pascal Charlier as he entered, accompanied by a nod from the uniformed officer who held the door open. With his polished demeanour, Pascal appeared unfazed, but the subtle tension in his shoulders betrayed his discomfort.

Beside Pascal Charlier, a figure whose presence seemed to illuminate the air around him, stood his press secretary, Antoine Lambert. This short, slim man, whom Léonie had observed the previous night at the law firm's party, clung to Pascal's side almost like a shadow. In stark contrast to Pascal's open and almost radiant persona, Antoine appeared closed off, his demeanour marked by a certain reluctance that seemed to erect an invisible barrier between himself and the rest of the world.

Pascal, with his easy charm and social grace, had a way of drawing people in. His laughter and bright conversations were like beacons in any gathering. He thrived in the spotlight, comfortable in his skin and in the roles he played, whether as a political leader or the life of the party. His charisma was undeniable, a trait that served him well both in political and social settings.

Antoine, on the other hand, presented a stark contrast. Even in the less formal setting of the meeting room, he seemed almost uncomfortable, as if the very act of being in his own skin was a constant challenge. Léonie remembered him from the party, how he had seemed more interested in the room than the people, his interactions forced, his smiles fleeting and somewhat strained. It was as if he was perpetually on the verge of retreating into himself, wary of the world and the people around him.

This dynamic between the two men was palpable, the differences in their personalities and approaches to the world underscoring the complexities of their relationship. Pascal, ever the politician, exuded a sense of openness and accessibility, while Antoine, the loyal confidante, remained an enigma, his true thoughts and feelings obscured behind a facade of professionalism.

The gravity of the conversation that was about to unfold seemed to weigh heavily on Antoine. Whereas Pascal appeared unfazed, ready to tackle whatever questions or accusations might come his way with his characteristic confidence and eloquence, Antoine seemed almost to shrink, his posture slightly hunched, as if bracing himself against an unseen storm.

Léonie invited her guests to take a seat with a welcoming and assertive gesture, bridging the gap between courtesy and the seriousness of their meeting.

The chairs, unlike the stark metal of an interrogation room, were padded yet offered little comfort given the circumstances.

As Pascal and Antoine settled, the light from the window caught the edges of Léonie's desk, highlighting the meticulous arrangement of her workspace. Every item, from the pen neatly placed atop an open notebook to the digital recorder poised for activation, spoke of her readiness to peel back the layers of Pascal's polished exterior.

With a glance at her notes, Léonie began, her voice steady, "Monsieur Charlier, I appreciate you making time for this today. I know these must be busy times for you, with the elections around the corner."

"Inspector Martens, I'm here to assist in any way I can," he replied, his voice smooth, practised. "We cannot let crime rule our precious streets, especially when an election is around the corner."

Antoine, silent, watched the exchange closely, ready to intervene but, for now, content to let Pascal lead their response.

"This isn't a formal questioning, but your insights could prove invaluable," Léonie continued her approach deliberate, designed to navigate the delicate balance between seeking cooperation and asserting her role in the investigation.

Pascal, aware of the stakes, nodded, his expression carefully neutral.

"We have some questions regarding the recent

murders of Dirk Meijer and Gaston Dupont and their connection to a certain painting," she said.

"Of course," Pascal replied, his voice steady. "If I can assist your investigation, Inspector."

"Your connection to Jean-Joseph Charlier is well-known, given your family ties," Léonie continued, her tone measured.

"We believe your ancestor is depicted in the painting," Léonie continued, her eyes flicking to Antoine momentarily, noting the subtle tightening of his jaw. "Are you certain that there is no family lore or hidden truths that might relate to these crimes?"

"Absolutely not," Pascal responded, the hint of frustration seeping into his tone. "My family has always been proud of our history and our ties to the Belgian Revolution, but we are not involved in the art world, nor do we hold any secrets that could explain these murders."

"Can you provide any insight into the significance of this painting?" Léonie pressed, observing Pascal's reactions closely.

Pascal paused, his brow furrowing in thought as he considered the question.

"I know that my ancestor was a hero of the Belgian Revolution and that his image may hold a certain power," he said slowly. "As for the painting itself, I was not aware of its existence till you told me. There are many paintings of our revolution hero." He smiled, showing off two rows of perfect white teeth. "But I am not an expert in art or history, Inspector. I cannot offer any insights into its true importance."

"Would it be possible for someone to use your family's name and legacy for their own nefarious purposes?" Léonie asked, her piercing green eyes searching for any signs of evasion.

"Anything's possible, Inspector," Pascal conceded, shifting uncomfortably in his seat."But I cannot fathom why someone would go to such lengths to involve my family in this."

12

The brisk air whipped at Nicolas De Wever's tailored coat as he strode with purpose towards the police station, its imposing stone casting a sombre shadow over the bustling square. His heart raced beneath his white shirt, and his mind buzzed with thoughts of his discoveries. These revelations could change Belgian history forever.

He and Isabella had parted ways, and she went back to the shop to attend to the last customers and tasks for the day as he pushed open the door to the police station.

"Excuse me," he called out urgently to the receptionist as he swept through the doors, his sharp blue eyes scanning the room for Inspector Léonie Martens. "I must speak with Inspector Martens immediately."

"Monsieur," the receptionist, a young man with spectacles, answered. "Please, wait in line for your turn."

"It is very urgent, I'm afraid," he replied tersely, barely acknowledging his presence. "I have crucial information for Léonie."

"Of course," the receptionist said with a smirk. "I'll see if she's available."

As the young man dialled a number and spoke in hush words, Nicolas took in the tense atmosphere that hung heavy in the air. Officers darted from one room to another, each seeming to carry the weight of their

investigations on their shoulders. The constant ringing
of phones punctuated the din, sending shivers down his
spine.

He clenched his jaw, his thoughts racing with the
implications of the cipher he had deciphered, the secrets
it held within its intricate script. Surely, Léonie would
understand the urgency of his mission and the need to
act swiftly before more lives were lost.

"Inspector Martens will be out shortly," the receptionist
announced, looking up at Nicolas again. "She asked that
you wait for her here."

"Thank you," Nicolas replied, nodding his gratitude.
His fingers drummed anxiously against his thigh, his
impatience growing with each passing moment.

The seconds ticked away like hours, his mind racing
with the secrets he carried and the lives that hung in
the balance.

The cacophony of ringing telephones and urgent
voices in the police station seemed to fade as the melodic
tones of a voice reached Nicolas's ears. He froze, his heart
skipping a beat as he recognised the dulcet timbre - it was
her, the elusive female decorator they had been searching
for. The puzzle pieces of their investigation were finally
falling into place, and he could feel the weight of destiny
pressing upon him.

"Excuse me," Nicolas whispered urgently to the
receptionist, his blue eyes alight with excitement. "I just
heard something… a voice of a person we've been looking

for… We need to tell Inspector Martens. Please go get her, now!"

The receptionist glanced around the crowded room and then back at Nicolas. "I'm sorry, Sir, but I can't leave my post. However, I shall inform Inspector Martens as soon as she's available."

"Make sure you do," Nicolas said, unable to keep the edge of impatience from creeping into his tone. He knew they were on the verge of solving this mystery, and every second that passed felt like an eternity.

He paced restlessly; each step betrayed his growing anticipation while his mind raced with the implications of their discoveries. This was not just about art and history anymore; it was about justice, about exposing the truth and holding those responsible accountable.

Police officers hurried to and fro, their determined strides echoing off the polished marble floor, while the constant ringing of telephones provided a concerto of urgency. Amidst this symphony of diligence stood Nicolas De Wever, his heart racing as he clutched the edge of the reception desk, his eyes fixed upon the door leading to the inner offices.

At last, the door opened, and Léonie emerged, her brow furrowed in concentration. Her piercing green eyes swept over the room, landing on Nicolas. She approached him, her stride a perfect blend of professionalism and practicality.

"Nicolas, what brings you here? This must be urgent."

"Indeed, it is, Léonie," Nicolas replied, a tremor of

excitement in his voice. "I just heard the voice of the decorator we've been searching for. She's here in the police station. We need to talk to her."

Léonie's eyes widened in surprise, and she glanced around the room as if expecting the elusive woman to materialise before them. "Are you certain? I have not seen any colourful women here today."

"Positive," Nicolas insisted, his blue eyes aflame with conviction. "I know her voice, and I am certain she is here, somewhere. We need to find her."

Léonie studied Nicolas for a moment, taking in his earnest expression and the unyielding determination that shone from his eyes. Léonie sighed, brushing a stray curl of blonde hair behind her ear.

"Very well," Léonie said, her voice firm but measured. "Nicolas, let us search the station. We cannot afford to lose this lead."

As they began their search, Nicolas couldn't help but feel a sense of anticipation building within him. The pieces of the puzzle were falling into place, and with each step, they drew closer to uncovering the truth. And though he knew the path ahead would be fraught with challenges, he could not deny the thrill that surged through him at the prospect of solving this enigmatic mystery once and for all.

Pascal Charlier emerged from the bathroom at the far end of the reception area, flanked by his press secretary.

"Inspector Martens, I hope I was of some assistance,"

Pascal greeted, his voice smooth and practised. The press secretary offered a polite smile in agreement.

"Monsieur Charlier," Léonie replied coolly, exchanging pleasantries without betraying her growing impatience. She cast a quick glance around the area, hoping to catch a glimpse of the elusive decorator. But there was no sign of her among the sea of faces.

Charlier greeted Nicolas with a broad smile that did not reach his eyes while the press secretary kept his eyes on the exit, looking like he really wanted to leave the station.

"Is there a problem, Inspector?" Pascal asked.

"Nothing that concerns you, Monsieur Charlier," Léonie replied, her tone firm yet measured. She was unwilling to divulge any information that might compromise their investigation.

"Very well," Pascal said, inclining his head in deference. He and the press secretary excused themselves, disappearing through the exit and leaving Léonie and Nicolas to continue their search in earnest.

"What was he doing here?" Nicolas asked.

"I've just interviewed him. A routine matter, as we talked about," Léonie replied. "So, where can this decorator be?" Léonie muttered under her breath, frustration evident in her voice. She opened the door to the back offices. The brightly lit, barren corridor echoed with the rhythmic tapping of Léonie's heels, her green eyes narrowing slightly as she regarded Nicolas with a mix of curiosity and confusion. The faint scent of oil paint lingered in the air, a subtle reminder of their foray into the art world.

As they traversed the bustling police station, weaving through officers and civilians alike, Nicolas's heart raced in tandem with his thoughts. It was fitting that the key to unravelling the enigma of the stolen art lay hidden amongst the people tasked with solving the mystery. The irony was not lost on him.

"Excuse me," Léonie addressed a young constable, halting their progress momentarily. "Have you seen a young woman, most likely dressed in very colourful clothing?"

"Can't say I have, Inspector," replied the constable, casting a cursory glance around the station before shaking his head.

"Thank you," Léonie said, frustration creeping into her tone. They continued their search, delving into every nook and cranny, but the elusive decorator remained just out of reach.

Why did this woman prove so challenging to find? Nicolas pondered, his brow furrowed in concentration. Was she aware they were searching for her, or was this a cruel twist of fate? Each passing moment only served to heighten his anxiety, and he could feel the weight of their responsibility bearing down upon him.

"This is futile," Léonie finally said. "She is not here. Either she slipped out unseen, or you were mistaken."

"I know I heard…" started Nicolas, but she interrupted him.

"You came here seeking me for another reason, yes?"

"Oh, yes. We have decoded the note," he said with a smile, and Léonie showed him to her desk.

*

Léonie's eyes narrowed as she leaned in closer, her voice laced with anticipation. "And what does it say?" she demanded, impatiently waiting for Nicolas to finish his tale of how they finally found the correct book to decode the mysterious note.

The light from the fluorescent lamps in the ceiling threw a cold, harsh light upon the parchment in front of Nicolas as his finger traced the intricate symbols of the cipher. The musty scent of ancient documents filled the air, mingling with the aroma of strong coffee that had long since gone cold. He could feel the tension in the room, thick and palpable as if they were on the cusp of a monumental discovery.

"Look," he whispered, unable to contain his excitement. "Here, the cipher reveals Jean-Joseph Charlier's actions during the Belgian Revolution. He apparently orchestrated some rather unscrupulous deals behind the scenes, betraying his comrades for personal gain."

Léonie's eyes widened as she examined the decoded message. "Are you certain? This could have grave consequences for our nation's history, not to mention Pascal Charlier's political career."

Nicolas nodded solemnly, his brow furrowed with

concern. "I am afraid so. It is all here, laid out in black and white."

"Mon Dieu," Léonie breathed, her hand trembling slightly as she brushed a stray lock of hair from her face. "To think that such an esteemed figure could be responsible for such duplicity... We cannot let this information go unacknowledged."

"Indeed," agreed Nicolas, his voice heavy with the weight of their discoveries. "We must confront Pascal Charlier about this, no matter how uncomfortable it may be."

"True," Léonie mused, her gaze drifting towards the window, where the last rays of sunlight cast long shadows across the polished floorboards. "However, Pascal has presented solid alibis for the time of both murders. We must tread carefully lest we accuse an innocent man."

"You need to question him again," demanded Nicolas.

In the meticulously ordered world of law enforcement, where evidence is the linchpin of justice, Inspector Léonie Martens and Nicolas De Wever found themselves navigating the treacherous waters of bureaucracy and scepticism. They stood before Chief Moreau to plea for revisiting Pascal Charlier with fresh questions.

The police chief, his expression a mask of professional detachment, listened as they laid out their case.

"The evidence against Charlier is purely circumstantial at this point," he pointed out, his voice bearing the weight of countless similar discussions. "You have no concrete link to the murders, no stolen painting in hand, and frankly, a political figure of Charlier's stature requires a solid case for any further questioning."

Feeling a surge of frustration, Nicolas interjected, "And what about my laptop, taken by the police as part of the investigation, that remains missing? It's not just an item of personal value—it contains critical information that could potentially link Charlier to the crimes."

The chief's gaze, steady and assessing, shifted between the antique dealer and his inspector. "A missing laptop, while unfortunate, doesn't constitute direct evidence. It's a loose thread in a tapestry of speculation."

Léonie, undeterred, leaned forward. "The only tangible link we have to the murderer, discovered in the locked room, is the bright yellow earring. It's distinctive, unusual, and we believe it belongs to the decorator—a key figure we're yet to identify."

The mention of the decorator piqued the chief's interest, his brow furrowing as he considered the implications.

"This decorator," he mused, "if indeed connected to Charlier, could be the missing piece you need. But without knowing who she is, your investigation is at a standstill."

The room fell into a thoughtful silence, the three of them caught in a moment of shared contemplation. It was clear that finding the decorator was not just a step but a leap towards unravelling the mystery that entangled Charlier, the stolen painting, and the murders.

Léonie and Nicolas exchanged a glance, a silent agreement passing between them.

"We understand the challenges," Léonie finally said, "but we're close, closer than we've ever been. Allowing us to question Charlier again could provide the breakthrough we need."

The chief leaned back, the lines of his face softening slightly. "I'll consider your request," he conceded, "but it is in the middle of the election campaigns, so I need more than just theories. Find me something solid, something undeniable, and you'll have my full support."

13

The sky over Brussels wore a veil of grey, a soft blanket that muted the colours of the city's waking streets. Within this subdued dawn, Nicolas De Wever found himself inside his antique shop, a sanctuary of history and memories. With its overcast but gentle day, the outside world seemed to press against the shop's windows, offering a quiet reminder of the world beyond.

Nicolas moved through the shop with familiarity, each step taking him past artefacts and heirlooms that spoke of eras long passed. Today, more than ever, he needed the comforting embrace of his shop's treasures, each item a bulwark against the tide of recent events that threatened to overwhelm him.

The crimes, the dark shadows that had been cast over his life, loomed at the edges of his thoughts. Yet, as he adjusted a display of vintage maps, Nicolas made a conscious effort to anchor himself in the present to the tangible objects that demanded his attention and care. The shop was his domain, a world where he could find respite from the storm of mysteries and accusations that had entangled him.

He paused before a newly acquired grandfather clock, its steady ticking a heartbeat in the quiet of the morning. The sound was comforting, a reminder of the continuity of time and the resilience of beauty. It was these moments, these tiny connections to the past, that Nicolas cherished most. They were a testament to his passion for antiques, a passion that had defined his life and career.

As the clock chimed, marking the hour, Nicolas's resolve solidified. Today, he would not allow the shadow of violence to darken his doorstep. He would greet his customers with the warmth and knowledge that had earned him respect in the antiques community. Today, he would be the guardian of history, the curator of stories that each piece in his collection carried.

With a deliberate sense of purpose, he turned the sign in the door's window to signal the shop's opening and unlocked the door. The small act felt like a ritual, marking the transition from the solitude of preparation to the anticipation of the day's visitors.

"Bon matin," chimed a distinguished gentleman who had been waiting patiently outside the door. He was impeccably dressed, sporting a tailored suit and cravat, exuding an aura of sophistication and refinement.

"Ah, good morning," smiled Nicolas. "How may I be of assistance to you today? Have you unearthed a hidden gem in need of my expertise?"

"Not really, but I am always on the lookout for unique pieces to add to my collection," the man replied as he strode further into the shop, his eyes scanning the shelves with practised discernment. "Your establishment never ceases to provide me with such delights."

Nicolas followed the gentleman's gaze, eager to share

his knowledge and passion for the antiques that filled the cosy space. His sharp blue eyes caught sight of a particular piece that he thought would pique the man's interest—an exquisite vase, its intricate design reflecting the artistry of skilled hands long past.

"Ah, I see you've noticed one of my latest acquisitions," Nicolas said, gesturing towards the vase. "A remarkable example of eighteenth-century porcelain from the famed Chantilly factory. Observe the delicate brush strokes depicting a pastoral scene, the soft hues of the enamels... Truly, a testament to the mastery of its creator."

The man leaned in closer, his fascination evident. "Magnificent," he murmured, gently tracing the rim of the vase with a reverent finger. "Such craftsmanship is a rarity these days. How much do you ask for this marvel, Monsieur?"

"Considering its provenance and impeccable condition, I believe a sum of 6,000 euros would be appropriate," Nicolas replied, his voice imbued with confidence and expertise.

"Very well, I shall take it," he declared without hesitation, clearly captivated by the antique. "Your eye for quality and knowledge of history never fails to impress me."

"Thank you," Nicolas answered, his heart swelling with pride as he carefully wrapped the vase in protective tissue paper. "It is always a pleasure to share my passion for the past with those who appreciate the beauty and significance of such treasures."

As the transaction was completed and the day's first customer departed with his newly acquired prize, Nicolas felt a familiar thrill of satisfaction. For him, there was no greater joy than connecting the artefacts of bygone eras with those who valued their historical importance–and, in doing so, preserving the stories that lay hidden within each antique for future generations to uncover.

The chime of the doorbell announced Isabella's arrival, her exuberant presence instantly illuminating the shop. She strode in with a lively gait, her dark tresses bouncing around her shoulders as she carried a tray of freshly brewed coffee.

"Good morning, Nicolas!" she called out cheerfully, her eyes sparkling with enthusiasm.

"Ah, Isabella," Nicolas replied, smiling at her infectious energy. He gratefully accepted the steaming cup from her outstretched hand, savouring the aroma of the rich, dark brew. "Your timing is impeccable, as always."

"Happy to help," Isabella beamed, setting the tray on the counter and rolling up her sleeves. "Now, what tasks do we have for today?"

Her nimble fingers got to work immediately, dusting off shelves, rearranging displays, and updating inventory records while humming a light tune under her breath. Nicolas couldn't help but admire her dedication and passion for the world of art and antiques, qualities that made her an invaluable assistant.

As they worked side by side, a sense of calm settled over the shop, the tranquillity only broken by the intermittent sound of the doorbell announcing new visitors. During one such lull, Inspector Léonie Martens entered, her usually confident stride faltering as she approached Nicolas, her brow furrowed with concern.

"Nicolas, I have thought about the locked room mystery," she said urgently, her voice low and tense. "I'm growing increasingly frustrated at our lack of progress in the investigation."

Nicolas set aside the delicate porcelain figurine he had been carefully cleaning and turned his full attention to Léonie.

"I share your frustration, Léonie. It's perplexing, to be sure. Let me get you a cup of coffee, and we'll discuss." He asked Isabella, "Will you take care of the shop for a while?"

Isabella nodded with a smile, and Nicolas took Léonie through to the backroom and his espresso machine.

"Espresso or cappuccino?" he enquired.

"Espresso, please... black as the shadows we're chasing," Léonie grinned, her piercing green eyes reflecting her disquiet. "Every lead seems to dissipate into thin air."

"Patience, my dear Inspector," Nicolas counselled gently, sipping his coffee as he contemplated the tangled threads of the mystery before them.

"Sometimes I wonder if we're overlooking something crucial," Léonie mused, running a hand through her short, curly blonde hair in frustration.

"Perhaps we are," Nicolas agreed thoughtfully, his gaze

drifting over the many treasures that filled his shop, each holding its own secret history. "But rest assured, we will unravel this enigma. After all, every locked room has a key, whether literal or metaphorical."

With those words of determination hanging between them, the pair resumed their investigation, their minds racing with possibilities and conjectures as they searched for the elusive truth hidden within the shadows of the art world.

"Could there be another way out?" Léonie asked, her voice tinged with both hope and scepticism. "An undiscovered door, perhaps?"

Nicolas thought about the building's layout, his sharp blue eyes scanning every nook and corner, searching for any sign of a hidden passage or secret entrance. His mind traced every wall and panel, considering any discrepancies that might betray a concealed exit.

"Or a window," Nicolas mused, his analytical mind racing as he considered each possibility. "We can't rule anything out. It's also possible that the killer remained inside the room when the police arrived, hidden from sight."

It was in this serene atmosphere that Claire Dubois entered, her poised figure wrapped in an elegant silk dress, its jewel-toned fabric shimmering like the iridescent wings of a rare butterfly.

"Ah, Claire," Nicolas greeted her, his voice as smooth. "Welcome back to my humble abode of antiquities."

Léonie, standing beside him, nodded in acknowledgement.

"Thank you, Nicolas," Claire responded with a gracious smile, her dark eyes gleaming with self-assured confidence. "I've just come from the exclusive gallery opening at the Palais des Beaux-Arts. Such a splendid event! I simply had to share the experience with you."

Nicolas's patience was wearing thin, the edges of his courtesy frayed by Clair's relentless barrage of stories, each more extravagant than the last. He had hoped for a brief encounter, an exchange of pleasantries at most, but Claire, oblivious to his growing disinterest, plunged ahead with her narrative.

"I really must insist, Claire," Nicolas attempted to interject, his tone laced with a polite yet firm desire to steer the conversation elsewhere. Yet, undeterred, Claire brushed aside his protests as if they were mere whispers in a gusty wind.

"Darling, you simply must hear about the gala," Claire pressed on, her enthusiasm undimmed. "The crème de la crème of the art world was there. Imagine rubbing shoulders with the Minister of Culture and the illustrious Luc Tuymans!" Her voice rose, infused with pride and excitement that seemed to fill the room, leaving little space for Nicolas's reservations.

Nicolas glanced at Léonie, seeking an ally in his silent plea for escape, but found her ensnared by Clair's storytelling, her attention seemingly captured by the vivid imagery Claire painted with her words.

"And the art, Nicolas! You should have seen the pieces on display. There was this portrait, oh! The luminosity of the subject's skin—it was like nothing I've ever seen before," Claire enthused, her hands gesturing as if to frame the artwork in the air between them.

With each word from Claire, Nicolas felt the urgency of their true purpose pressing against the confines of the polite conversation. He remembered the critical piece of information that had momentarily slipped his mind, a detail that could pivot their investigation in a new direction. This recollection gnawed at him, urging him to cut through the opulence of Clair's recollections.

As Clair's narrative wove through the grandeur of the gala, Nicolas found his opening. "Claire, that's fascinating, but we really must discuss—" he started, only to be swept aside by Clair's relentless tide of storytelling.

"Ah, but you must let me finish, Nicolas. The ambience, the people, the art—it was a night to remember!" Claire insisted, her determination to share her experience overshadowing Nicolas's attempts to redirect the conversation.

The urgency within Nicolas surged, a stark contrast to the leisurely pace of Clair's gala tales. He realised then that Claire, with her stories of art and high society, was not just oblivious to his discomfort but entirely focused on her own narrative, her need to share overshadowing the cues of her audience.

As Claire continued her vivid narration, a sudden flicker of urgency sparked within Nicolas. He recalled a crucial detail that had slipped his mind during their earlier discussions. Abruptly, he interrupted Claire, his voice edged with a newfound intensity.

"Claire, forgive me for cutting short your fascinating account, but I must ask you about something of great importance." His sharp blue eyes bored into hers, demanding her full attention. "Do you remember what you said to me right after Dirk Meijer's murder?"

As she met his gaze with a blank stare, Nicolas continued: "You said to me that the police came back. What made you say that?"

Clair's brow furrowed in thought as she recalled the incident.

"Ah, yes. It was rather peculiar," she sighed, her voice tinged with unease. "A uniformed officer had come by while you were away, and Dirk was still here. I didn't think much of it at the time."

Léone took a step forward, her expression intense. "Did you notice anything unusual about the officer? Anything at all?"

Claire paused momentarily, her hazel eyes scanning the room as if looking for answers. "Nothing out of the ordinary," she finally replied, her voice quiet but resolute. "He was rather small in stature, almost frail-looking. But beyond that, there was nothing suspicious about him." The words sounded hollow to Clair's ears; something about the officer had set her on edge, but she couldn't quite put her finger on it.

"Anything else?" Léonie pressed. "Skin colour? Hair colour?"

"I only saw his back, but I do remember thinking his uniform appeared to be somewhat ill-fitting. But I guess it is hard to find standard sizes for such a delicate body…"

"Thank you, Madame Dubois," Léonie said, her voice measured yet firm. "Your observation may prove to be invaluable to our investigation."

"An ill-fitting uniform," Nicolas mused aloud, his fingers tapping thoughtfully on the polished surface of the antique table before him. "Could it be that our mysterious officer is not what he appears to be?"

In this intricate web of deception and secrets, one thing became clear: the key to unravelling the locked room mystery lay within their reach, and with each step closer, the truth would slowly emerge from the darkness.

"Are you suggesting that someone disguised themselves as a police officer?" Léonie asked, the realisation dawning on her face.

"It's possible," Nicolas confirmed, excitement rising in his chest. "If our true culprit had access to a police uniform disguised as an officer, he could have concealed themselves within the shop until the police arrived, only to slip away when the opportunity presented itself."

"Plausible," Léonie whispered, her eyes wide with admiration for Nicolas's analytical prowess. "This could be the crucial lead we've been searching for!"

"Indeed," agreed Nicolas, his heart pounding in

anticipation of what this new revelation could mean for their investigation.

"But what about the earring and the decorator?" Léonie said as Claire said goodbye to Isabella and left the shop.

"Yes, we must find the flamboyant decorator," Nicolas conceded.

Isabella, who had been quietly rearranging some eighteenth-century statuettes near the counter, suddenly looked up, her expression alight with a realisation.

"You know, I think I've seen her... or rather, him," she said, her voice tinged with surprise and certainty.

Nicolas and Léonie paused, their attention shifting to Isabella as if magnetised by the potential breakthrough her words suggested.

"At a pride party at the university," Isabella continued, her eyes reflecting the vivid memories of the event. "He was in drag, dressed so flamboyantly that you couldn't help but notice him. The colours, the fabrics—it was all so... dazzling."

Nicolas blinked, the information settling in his mind with the weight of a revelation. "I never realised," he murmured, a sense of astonishment weaving through his words. "The colourful clothing... it's designed to draw the eye away from the obvious. That she is, in fact, a he."

Léonie leaned in, her detective's mind piecing together the implications.

"So, the person we've been looking for, the one buying antiques from you, Nicolas, under the guise of a decorator... appearances may have misled us. This individual, comfortable in the spotlight at a pride event, could easily navigate the art and antique world without arousing suspicion."

Isabella nodded, her observation bringing a new dimension to their investigation.

"Exactly. And thinking back, there was something about him... a confidence, an air of someone used to disguising their true intentions. It's not just about the drag; it's about using that persona as a mask, a way to blend in or stand out at will."

While processing this new information, Nicolas felt a mix of admiration and frustration. "All this time, the flamboyant clothing, the bold choices... they weren't just personal style. They were a diversion, a way to keep us from seeing the truth hiding in plain sight."

Though stunned by the turn of events, Nicolas felt a renewed sense of purpose. The decorator, a character as complex as any piece in his shop, had the ability to take on a different form, maybe even any form.

"Léonie," he said with a steady voice, "I think I know. We need to see the Chief."

14

The interview room was eerily quiet, save for the soft rustle of paper as Inspector Léonie Martens and Nicolas De Wever took their seats across from Pascal Charlier, the controversial nationalist politician, and his press secretary, Antoine Lambert. The bright fluorescent lights above cast harsh shadows on their faces, making them seem almost otherworldly.

"Monsieur Charlier," Léonie began, leaning forward, her green eyes piercing through the silence like emerald daggers. "Are you familiar with Dirk Meijer and Gaston Dupont?"

"Only by reputation," Pascal replied promptly, his gaze unwavering. "Their work in the art world is well known, but I had no personal relationship with either of them."

"Indeed," Léonie mused, making a note in her pad. "And yet, we have reason to believe there may be a connection between you and the victims. Where were you during the time of Dirk Meijer's murder?"

Pascal Charlier straightened his posture, his face a defiant mask. "I was attending a fundraiser, Inspector. I have numerous witnesses who can attest to my whereabouts that night," he said, his voice steady and confident.

Léonie's gaze never wavered as she studied him, her mind racing with questions and possibilities. She turned briefly to Nicolas, whose blue eyes seemed almost to glow in the dim light, betraying his sharp focus. She noted the subtle tightening of his jaw as if he, too, sensed that something wasn't quite right.

"Interesting," Léonie mused aloud, returning her attention to Pascal. "And what of your connection to Gaston Dupont, the art forger? As you know, your family's history is tied to the man in the painting, Jean-Joseph Charlier."

"Well," Pascal nodded, though his tone was guarded, "Jean-Joseph Charlier, or 'Wooden Leg', as he was known, was a hero of the Belgian Revolution. He happens to be a distant relative of mine." He paused as if weighing his next words carefully. "However, I assure you, Inspector, I never have had any dealings with this Monsieur Dupont. I have no interest in forgeries."

"Monsieur Charlier," she continued, her voice steady and matter-of-fact, "can you please confirm your whereabouts during the time of Gaston Dupont's murder?"

Pascal straightened his tie, a bead of sweat glistening on his temple. "Certainly, Inspector," he replied smoothly, exuding an air of confidence that belied the gravity of the situation. "As I have previously stated, I was at a rally for my political party, surrounded by numerous witnesses." Pascal's eyes flickered momentarily towards Antoine Lambert before he continued, "You know there is a national election in just a few months, 68 days to be exact."

His press secretary looked at his watch as if to see if the day count was correct and then nodded.

"Yet, your association with the painting and its connection to the murders raises questions", Léonie pressed on, her voice firm but not accusatory.

"I understand your need to explore every avenue, Inspector, but I assure you, my relationship with this stolen painting has no bearing on these terrible crimes."

"Very well, Mr. Charlier," Léonie conceded, her mind already leaping ahead to the next line of inquiry. "We appreciate your cooperation." She cast a meaningful glance at Nicolas, whose own suspicions had been piqued by their conversation.

Nicolas found himself unable to tear his gaze away from Antoine Lambert. He watched intently as the man's slender fingers twisted a handkerchief into knots, betraying a restless energy that belied his seemingly calm exterior. His slicked-back hair and thin frame only served to heighten the sense of unease that Nicolas felt in his presence.

"Inspector Martens," Nicolas said, his blue eyes reflecting the intensity of his thoughts. "May I ask a question?"

"By all means," Léonie replied, giving him a nod of approval.

"Mr. Lambert," Nicolas began, turning his attention to the press secretary, his words measured and deliberate. "You seem rather nervous. Is there something you wish to share with us?"

Antoine's eyes widened momentarily as if caught off guard by the sudden shift in focus. He swallowed hard as he struggled to find his voice. "I... I'm just concerned about Pascal, the election… our votes…, that's all," he stammered.

"Tell me," Léonie took over, "did you accompany Monsieur Charlier to these events?"

Upon turning her attention toward Pascal Charlier's press secretary, Léonie scrutinised the short, thin man sitting silently beside his master. His slicked-back hair reflected the room's harsh lighting. His nervous demeanour was apparent as he fidgeted with the cuff of his sleeve. The contrast between him and the confident, assertive party leader was striking.

"Absolutely," Antoine responded after a brief hesitation, his eyes flicking back and forth between Léonie and Pascal. "He was attending a charity gala at the Royal Museum of Fine Arts, along with several other members of his staff."

As Nicolas heard Lambert's answers, he got the confirmation he needed, not so much in the words as in the voice.

"Mr. Lambert," Nicolas cut in, his voice steady despite the turmoil churning within him, "ever since the murder of Dirk Meijer, we've searched for a decorator, a very colourful decorator whose earring was found on the scene of the crime. Listening to you talking, I'm sure she is none other than you."

Antoine Lambert flinched, and even Pascal's

expression flickered, the only sign of disturbance in his otherwise composed facade.

"That's a serious accusation. Do you have evidence to support such a claim?" His voice was calm and measured, but an undercurrent of caution lay beneath it.

Nicolas leaned forward, the pieces of the puzzle laid out before him.

"Not only did you disguise yourself to purchase antiques from my shop, but you returned, hidden behind the uniform of a police officer, to steal a painting. A painting that, if revealed, could severely damage your party's credibility and, consequently, the election results."

Léonie interjected, her gaze fixed on Lambert, "And then there's the matter of Gaston Dupont's murder. The art forger who knew too much about the original painting, the one that could expose the truth behind your party's facade."

"You've been seen at the University's pride party, Mr. Lambert. Your ability to transform, to blend in or stand out at will... It's impressive, but it also makes you the perfect candidate for such a role. The flamboyant attire, the elaborate disguises—it all points to you."

Lambert's mask began to crack, the allegations and the evidence laid bare, leaving little room for denial. "You think dressing up for a party makes me capable of theft and murder?" There was a hint of defiance in his tone, a challenge to the narrative being constructed around him.

Nicolas met his gaze, unflinching. "It's not just about the clothing or the parties. It's about motive, opportunity, and behaviour. You had a lot to gain from keeping the painting hidden."

The room fell silent, the weight of the moment settling heavily upon its occupants. Lambert, now the centre of suspicion, seemed to shrink slightly, the reality of his situation dawning upon him. Yet, defiance still sparkled in his eyes, a testament to the battle of wits and wills unfolding.

"But… but why would I?" he stammered.

The silence that permeated the room was suddenly shattered by the sharp creak of the door swinging open. A gust of cold air ushered in Chief Moreau, his face a stern tableau chiselled from years of unyielding dedication to justice. His authoritative presence seemed to fill every corner of the interrogation chamber, casting an undeniable weight upon its occupants.

"Inspector Martens, Mr. De Wever," he said curtly, nodding towards Léonie and Nicolas. "I have news that might be of interest to you both."

Léonie raised a questioning eyebrow, her lips pursed with anticipation. "What is it, Chief?"

Moreau held forward a package wrapped in white. The faintest trace of a smile played at the corners of Chief Moreau's mouth as he slowly unfurled a white cloth. Cold and unyielding as steel, his eyes bored into Antoine Lambert, who shrank beneath his gaze.

The room seemed to hold its breath, the tense air thick with anticipation and unspoken revelations.

"Mr. Lambert," the Chief began, his voice heavy with

the weight of impending justice, "allow me to present the pièce de résistance - the missing painting recovered in pristine condition." He paused for effect, allowing the gravity of the situation to settle upon Antoine's slender shoulders. "And, as an added bonus, Mr. De Wever's laptop, which we discovered hidden alongside the artwork."

Antoine's eyes widened, darting between the painting and the laptop, his mind racing to comprehend the damning evidence laid before him. Nicolas observed the press secretary closely, noting the way his hands trembled ever so slightly, betraying the composed facade he desperately fought to maintain.

"What does this have to do with Antoine?" burst Pascal.

"It was found in his wardrobe, along with a substantial collection of women's clothing."

*

In the quietude of Nicolas's shop, where every shadow seemed steeped in history and every gleam of light whispered of bygone eras, Nicolas De Wever and Inspector Léonie Martens found themselves ensnared in a labyrinth of theories and revelations. The room, surrounded by relics of the past, served as a fitting backdrop for their deliberation on a mystery that had trapped them both in its complex web.

Léonie, her gaze sharp and thoughtful, broke the silence. "The murders, the locked room—it's like something out of a classic mystery novel, yet here we are, living it. Lambert's role in this... it's almost unfathomable."

Nicolas, leaning against an ancient oak desk, nodded solemnly.

"Yes, Lambert's actions have cast a long shadow over everything we thought we knew. Dressing as a decorator, embracing his feminine side to blend in, then returning as a police officer to claim what he believed was his... It's a tale too convoluted for fiction, yet here we are."

"The painting," Léonie continued, piecing together the puzzle with methodical precision, "it was the linchpin. Upon seeing the old painting he commissioned to be painted over within these walls, Lambert must have been distraught. His actions were those of a man desperate to preserve a secret, a secret so damaging that murder became an acceptable risk."

"Yes," Nicolas sighed, the weight of the situation pressing down upon him. "Lambert had the original painting covered up, obliterated by another layer of paint. It's as if he believed he could simply erase the past, along with its truths."

Léonie nodded, her mind racing with the implications. "And it wasn't just the painting. Lambert himself, disguising in women's clothing to act out as a decorator or party with the drags at university, is all part of the same pattern. He hides behind layers, be it paint or fabric, all to maintain a facade."

The air between them was charged with the gravity of their insights.

"It's desperation," Léonie continued, "a desperate attempt to cover up anything that might cast a shadow over the elections, over the image he's worked so hard to cultivate. But why? What is it about the painting, about his actions, that he believes could be so detrimental?"

Nicolas, leaning forward, his elbows on his knees, looked thoughtful. "It's the fear of exposure, isn't it? Lambert is terrified of anything that might challenge the narrative he's constructed or reveal the cracks in the persona he presents to the world."

"His actions, they're not just about political strategy," Léonie mused, her gaze distant as she pieced together the psychological puzzle that was Antoine Lambert. "They're about control, about dictating the narrative at any cost. And when that control is threatened, he reacts. The murder of Gaston, the theft of the painting, it's all reactionary, a man lashing out to keep his secrets buried."

Nicolas sighed. "It's tragic, in a way. In his quest to avoid shame, Lambert has only succeeded in weaving a tighter web around himself, one that's bound to unravel. And Dirk Meijer, an innocent caught in the crossfire of Lambert's desperation. To think, Lambert hid in the back office, cloaked in the anonymity of a technician's overall, slipping out amidst the chaos with the painting, documents, and my laptop. It's a boldness born of necessity. And Gaston..."

Léonie's expression hardened at the mention of

Gaston Dupont. "Gaston's murder was the final act of a man cornered by his own deeds. Killing the art forger who knew the truth about the original painting was Lambert's way of tying up loose ends, a desperate attempt to cover his tracks."

The room around them, filled with objects, each bearing its own silent testament to the passage of time, seemed to resonate with the gravity of their conversation. The solution to the locked room mystery, a narrative woven with desperation, identity, and betrayal, lay bare before them, a testament to their perseverance and acumen.

"As we piece together Lambert's journey through this tragedy, from decorator to murderer, it's clear that the painting was more than just art; it was a catalyst for a series of events that spiralled beyond anyone's control," Nicolas mused, his voice a blend of sorrow and determination.

Léonie, standing up, her resolve mirrored in her posture, spoke with a renewed sense of purpose. "Now it's up to the prosecution and the legal system to bring Lambert to justice."

EPILOGUE

The sun cast a golden glow on the KBR museum's exterior. Amidst the hushed whispers of the museum's visitors, Nicolas and Léonie stood side by side, their gazes locked on the carefully restored items behind glass as they were displayed at its place of honour. The air around them felt charged with anticipation, the walls seeming to hum with the weight of history.

"Can you believe we're finally here?" Léonie asked a hint of wonder in her voice.

"Hardly," Nicolas admitted, his gaze never leaving the case. "To think that this masterpiece has been hidden for so long, its true historical significance is nearly lost forever."

"And this is the perfect place for it," she said.

"Yes, the book that pushed us toward the solution is here, and the story of the encrypted note in the secret compartment in the frame makes this artwork unique."

"Indeed," Léonie smiled. "And the story doesn't seem to alter Belgium First's chances in the elections."

"No, Charlier is in the media more than ever before…"

She turned to face him, her expression softening. "Nicolas, you took risks beyond what was expected, and you never wavered in your pursuit of justice. I am truly grateful to have had you by my side during this quest."

"Well," Nicolas agreed, his blue eyes reflecting the

intensity of his thoughts. "We faced many challenges along the way, yet we persevered."

As they continued to observe the painting, Nicolas marvelled at the depth of emotion that seemed to radiate from every brushstroke. It was as if the artist had poured their soul onto the canvas, leaving a testament to their skill and passion. At that moment, he felt an overwhelming sense of awe and humility, acutely aware of his responsibility as a steward of such a priceless treasure.

"Every brushstroke, every pigment," Nicolas murmured, his voice barely audible, "tells a story that spans generations. And we, Léonie, have played our part in ensuring those stories live on."

"Yes," she agreed, her voice equally low, almost reverent. "In a way, we have become guardians of these forgotten chapters of Belgian history."

As they turned to leave, the echoes of their footsteps mingled with the whispers of the past, creating a symphony of triumph and discovery that would resonate long after they had departed.

THE END

A story from

Yesteryear's stories reflected today
Yabot AB
www.yabot.se